An Eagle
Amongst
The Ravens

David Jowsey

First published 2022
by David Jowsey Books

Cover image by David Jowsey
© David Jowsey 2022
All rights reserved

Typeset in: 10/13pt Jansen

ISBN 13: 9798807412010

A catalogue record for the first edition
of this book is available from the British Library.

For Mam and Dad,

With love

Prologue
June 13th, 1940

By the time the first bombs fell the children were on their way. Some saw it as an adventure, others as torture. Many never saw home again. But for everyone, it was an experience that would change their lives forever.

Mr Hitler saw to that

The first children had been evacuated in the summer of 1939 as Britain declared war on Germany. Now, as enemy forces amassed along the French coastline and the Luftwaffe prepared to blitz cities across the country with devastating bombing raids, the time to evacuate the remaining children had come. It was never going to be easy.

The station felt claustrophobic, its windows crisscrossed with tape, its doorways framed by sandbags. It felt cold and unfriendly, its platform crowded with bewildered and frightened families, cardboard suitcases and brown-paper parcels cluttered between them. Their final moments together were all they had left to sustain one another over the coming months, but such moments would never be enough.

A ripple of desperation spread across the platform as the crowd bustled into activity. Teachers ushered children towards open carriage doors, hesitant to break up final embraces, but aware of the need to depart. This was the moment that had filled so many with dread.

Peggy's voice was thick with emotion but Robert remained silent. He wasn't sure how his voice would sound if he spoke and he forced his own emotions deep into his chest, desperate not to allow his feelings to betray him. It was a belief his father had instilled in him from a young age and he was desperate not to let his father down. He inhaled deeply and coughed to cover the flutter that sat high up behind his ribs.

Mother planted a lingering kiss upon each of their foreheads, her smile forced, the corners of her mouth tight. She wiped a black smudge from her son's face and tightened the ribbons in her daughter's hair one final time before straightening her hat.

'You're going to have such a wonderful time.' Her words were strained, her voice little more than a croak with the force of emotion. 'You have all your school friends with you and you have each other.' She forced another smile. 'You'll barely notice the days pass.'

Robert's chin trembled and he bit his lip as he forced back the tears. Their mother had endured so much in recent months, with their father away fighting and now the impending threat of invasion. Her nerves had begun to show themselves more openly and it had been hard for Peggy and Robert not to notice. 'There's really no need to send us away.' Robert spoke as calmly as he could manage and found his voice strengthening with every word. 'We can stay here with you.' He looked to his sister for support. 'We want to.' Peggy shook her head. *Robert, please don't do this.*

Mother kissed him again and ran her fingers gently over his face, savouring the touch of his skin. 'I know, and I do want you to stay.' She looked between them both. 'I want you both to stay, but it's just the way it has to be.' She licked her thumb and rubbed again at the stubborn mark upon his cheek until it faded. Despite his protest, she held him fast until she was satisfied he was as clean as she could make him, then cupped his face between her hands. 'Robert, we've talked about this. It's for your own good.' She paused before adding, 'and your safety.'

Their mother had said it so many times since the order to evacuate had been issued, and Peggy wondered whether she had been attempting to convince herself as much as she had them. At that moment, as they stood alongside the train, the reality of leaving home was more than either of them could bear. It seemed so real, so final. She wrapped her arms around her son and opened an arm for her daughter to join them. Her final hug was so powerful it told them she did not expect to see her children for a very long time.

Turning them to face the train, she urged Robert towards the outstretched hand of his teacher. He suddenly looked small and young in his too-big overcoat, its sleeves burying his hands until only his fingers were visible, his knees white between the hem of the coat and the tops of his woollen socks. His gas mask case hung around his neck, bulky and obtrusive, and Miss Danby rearranged it so it hung under his arm before she took his parcel of belongings and led him reluctantly towards the carriage. Mother delicately stroked her daughter's face one final time. 'Look after him,' she whispered, and with a final touch, she ushered Peggy onwards.

The corridor was barely wide enough for two people to stand side by side. Peggy held onto her brother's shoulders as she urged him forward, her body tense and unwilling, the contact between them strengthening her determination not to turn back. If it was not for the bodies that closed in behind them she felt sure one of them would have turned and bolted.

A narrow door led into a compartment where seats lined the walls to either side. Suitcases and paper parcels lay discarded across them as bodies rushed to fill the window. Desperate cries and pleas to stay filled the air and Peggy forced her brother into a gap from where he could view the platform. She stood behind him, her hands on his shoulders, her extra height meaning she had only to crane her neck a little to see, but if the train was to pull away before they saw mother for the final time...

Mother stood a little way back amidst the crowd, her form thin and shrunken, and Robert's strength left him at the sight of her. The emotions he had struggled so hard to force back, the tears he had kept buried finally surfaced, and he wailed. Peggy gripped his hand but he did not squeeze back. He seemed unaware of anything other than the mother he so desperately loved, out there before him on the station platform.

A whistle shrieked and the carriage shuddered as doors slammed along its length. The train gave a lurch and mother waved confidently, but her arm faltered momentarily and the painted-on smile she had worn all morning collapsed into a sorrow Peggy had not seen before. Smoke and steam covered her, and in an instant she was gone.

Peggy knew she had to be strong for her brother; she had promised, but the world suddenly erupted into a blur and she could hold back no longer. Emotions took hold as they pressed their faces to the cold glass, and as the steam momentarily parted they caught a final glimpse. Mother looked old and frail, a broken ghost of the woman she had been, and Peggy closed her eyes in an attempt to replace the vision with the woman she knew she was. When she opened them again the station platform had vanished.

Peggy stood for a while, consumed by her own emotions before she calmed herself enough to coax her brother away from the window. He sat motionless beside her, his face a mask of disbelief, and she smoothed his hair as her distress bubbled just beneath the surface. The look on their mother's face would remain with Peggy for the rest of her days.

The carriage gradually quietened as their teacher moved between them, offering an encouraging word here, a gentle smile there. Miss Danby was a kindly woman in her late twenties whose natural poise was graceful and elegant, and not unlike that of a ballet dancer to Peggy's way of thinking. She was also not as aloof as other teachers, taking a little more interest in her pupils than some thought appropriate. It reflected now as she, too, appeared affected by the emotion of their leaving.

As tears faded, conversations about what may await them took hold. For many, the anxiety of separation would turn to curiosity and excitement as a new world unveiled itself at the end of their journey, while others would be met with a cold welcome devoid of love or wanting.

Peggy looked at her brother's sleeping form in the seat alongside her. She could only hope that what awaited them would be the world they so desperately needed, a world to replace the one they left behind.

How wrong she would be.

Chapter 1

Mrs Barnforth did not want them, that much was obvious. While other children were welcomed by the strangers who were to be their guardians for the coming months, Robert and Peggy were left to sit in a corner of the village hall until she was ready.

A stern-faced lady of middling years, Mrs Barnforth presented a brash and no-nonsense manner to which they would quickly become accustomed. She wore a plain but meticulously hand-stitched green dress matched with a tweed jacket, white lace-trimmed gloves and a felt hat held in place by an oversized hat-pin. She eyed the children coldly from the moment she stepped through the doorway, her first words to the Billeting Officer deliberately loud and unfeeling.

'I take it they are the children I am to have?' She raised her brow as she studied the girl and her brother in cold disgust. 'Quite an untrustworthy looking pair, I must say.' She turned her back on them as she faced an older lady with a clipboard. 'And I suppose they have head lice?' she said, deliberately raising her voice so they heard every word. 'The last thing I want is for my girls to catch such a disgusting condition from the likes of - '

Mrs Forsyth, the Billeting Officer for the village of Ravenscroft, a small farming village just to the north of Whitby, interrupted Mrs Barnforth. A strong character in her own right with a well-defined sense of right and wrong, Mrs Forsyth's dislike for the woman known within village circles as 'Bolshy Barnforth' was evident in her manner. It was not without good reason, for the village's most conceited resident did little to hide her wealth and self-promoted position on the Parish Council, much to the disdain of other parishioners. While she regularly had something to say about matters, whether they were of concern to her or not, her views were often unwelcome.

'Peggy and Robert Cotterill, eleven and ten years respectively, from Middlesbrough,' stated Mrs Forsyth with an undisguised tone of contempt for her visitor. 'Father is away fighting, mother is working in a munitions factory.' She paused briefly, proud of the contribution both parents were making towards the war effort, and considerably more than Mrs Barnforth had made in recent months, unless one counted telling those around her what to do. 'And whether or not they have head lice is your concern, Mrs Barnforth.' She made an over-dramatic show of ticking off both children's names from her list. 'After all, you seem to be more than competent at keeping your own girls clear.'

Mrs Barnforth spared the Billeting Officer the sharp end of her tongue. It appeared the two ladies had crossed words on numerous occasions, but this was not to be the next. Instead, Mrs Barnforth pierced the children with a menacing stare as they huddled in the corner, a mild early evening chill nipping at their tired faces. When they did not instantly jump into motion Mrs Barnforth clicked her fingers. 'Come on then,' she snapped. 'Chop-chop! Do you think I have all night?'

The journey to their new home took place in silence. Neither child dared speak, and Mrs Barnforth made no attempt to involve them in any form of conversation. Instead, she slammed her foot down upon the clutch and rammed the car into gear with more force than seemed necessary, taking corners like an angry hornet and cursing other locals who dared to cross her path.

The car was one of only a few owned locally, its bottle-green paintwork and gleaming chrome widely despised by all on account of its driver. She raced now through the marketplace, narrowly avoided a collision with a startled elderly gentleman who passers-by hauled from the car's path, and sped on with scant regard for anyone other than herself. Peggy risked a hurried glance behind her in time to witness the shocked faces of onlookers and saw fists raised in annoyance.

It seemed, despite the dangers of Mrs Barnforth's driving and the fury of her mood, that for the moment the children were in the safest place.

Early evening dusk hid much of the detail as they sped out of the village. Trees lined the road as the car sped along, before falling away to a blur of hedges that gave an impression of openness beyond.

Peggy and Robert sat rigid on the back seat, their eyes wide in alarm as the car hurtled them further into the deepening twilight. Peggy felt cold fingers slide into hers and she looked down to find Robert's hand, the contact unexpected, and she curled her fingers around his.

The car turned off the road without slowing and passed through an open gate amid a flurry of noise and activity. Chickens clucked and squawked in fright as the car whipped through them with no concern for injury or death, and with a sudden application of the brakes, Mrs Barnforth pulled the car to a halt. She slammed its door behind her with unconcealed fury and stomped away. The car fell silent.

'Are we here?' whispered Robert. His voice was small and frail, his eyes wide with concern.

Peggy shrugged. When Mrs Barnforth did not return she assumed they were meant to go up to the house and grasped the handle of her suitcase. She felt around in the darkness for the lever to open the door, but never having been in a car before she didn't know whether to pull or push. To her surprise, the door swung open.

A pungent smell filled their nostrils and Robert nipped at his nose. He recoiled and pulled his jumper over

11

his mouth. 'That stinks!' he said and coughed as the smell caught in his throat. 'Phwoar!' he growled. 'Smells like poo!'

Peggy laughed. 'We're in the countryside now. I suppose we'll just have to get used to it.' She clambered down from the back seat, a scattering of noise and movement causing her to jump and she shrieked in alarm before erupting into a fit of giggles. 'Chickens,' she said with a grin, her first natural smile for days.

Robert shuffled across the seat and glanced outside. 'Come on,' Peggy said, 'they won't hurt you.' She grabbed for her brother's hand and together they stepped out onto the cobbles.

The ground was hard and uneven, the buildings ahead and to the right mere blocks of shadow framed by the overhanging darkness of towering trees. To the left ran a fence, beyond which it appeared the world had vanished. Something moved in the darkness and a rustle, followed by a huge snort, signalled a presence in the shadows. A shape hung its head over the fence and they jumped, startled by the horse's sudden appearance. It snorted again and nodded as though laughing at them.

Everything about the world appeared over-large and out of proportion, the sky a vast openness filled with more stars than either of them had imagined possible. They glimmered like scattered diamonds, a million pinpoints that filled the dome of the night. There were certainly far more than could be seen from the streets of Middlesbrough, and Peggy nudged her brother, their horsey visitor momentarily forgotten as they stared in amazement at the unfolding night.

Their wonder was broken by the squeal of hinges. A rectangle of light opened in the darkness and a silhouette filled the open doorway. It wasn't long before a voice boomed across the farmyard.

'If you two want to stand out there gawping all night then go ahead, but I will be locking this door at nine sharp. If you're not inside, don't expect me to wait around for you!'

Peggy and Robert stood in the hallway. The mat beneath their feet was as large as their kitchen table at home but coarse like a yard broom. It was nothing like the Clippy mats they had made from scraps of fabric with their mother.

The hallway towered above them and Robert pressed his shoulder into Peggy's side. She could sense his nervousness as he stared along the carpeted hallway. It was dimly lit and stretched between walls of dark panelled wood which seemed to vanish into nothingness. A spindled bannister rail lined the staircase as it rose to the left and an ornate lamp hung from the ceiling above, while a table stood against one wall with an oil lamp and a telephone upon it. The hallway smelt of polish, a welcome relief from the farmyard smells that had greeted them outside. It looked as though it had never seen a speck of dust.

Mrs Barnforth eyed them both with mistrust and they immediately felt uncomfortable. Peggy resisted the urge to shuffle, but Robert could not help himself. When he dropped his head Mrs Barnforth told him to Stand up straight! and Peggy sensed her brother tremble beneath the glare.

Opening a door into another room, whoever Mrs Barnforth spoke to was deserving of a different tone, her words towards them loving and warm. In response, twin girls not much older than Peggy stepped into the hallway. 'These are my daughters,' said Mrs Barnforth. Both were dressed in their nightdresses and dressing gowns, their hair tied with ribbons in readiness for bed. She placed a loving arm around the taller girl's shoulders. 'This is Veronica,' she said with obvious pride, before placing an arm around the smaller girl's shoulders. 'And this is Vivienne.' The girls gave weak smiles. Neither girl convinced Peggy they meant it.

'Now, we have rules in this house, don't we girls?' said Mrs Barnforth.

Veronica and Vivienne nodded as one. 'Yes, Mother.'

'And what is the first rule of the house?' Mrs Barnforth asked.

'No running around or making noise,' answered Veronica.

Well, that's Robert in trouble for a start, Peggy thought. She bit her tongue and shifted her weight slightly to one side to nudge up against her brother. *Are you listening?* the movement said.

'Very good,' said Mrs Barnforth. 'Now, rule number two: shoes are not allowed on the carpets. We take them off at the door and put on our carpet slippers before entering the house.' She indicated our current footwear. 'You do have carpet slippers, I take it?' she asked judgingly.

'Yes,' Peggy said quietly. Mother had packed her own, but Robert's had seen better days. Somehow Peggy did not think either pair would be good enough to wear around Mrs Barnforth's home.

'Well, that's something,' said Mrs Barnforth scathingly. She pointed out a series of doors one at a time. 'You are allowed in the living room, the kitchen and the breakfast room, but not the parlour.' She turned to indicate a single door at the end of the hall. 'And at the back of the house is Professor Barnforth's study. Under no circumstances should you ever enter that room, and make no mistake, there shall be dire consequences should I ever find out you have done so.'

Peggy swallowed hard. Was this meant to be a safe place away from the bombs? Maybe it had been better to stay at home after all.

Mrs Barnforth pointed to the mat beneath their feet. 'You will remove your outer garments where you stand. Coats must be hung neatly, shoes beneath, gas masks easily accessible on top. Carpet slippers must always be put on before you step into the house. On this occasion, I shall allow you to walk around in your stocking feet until you have unpacked, after such time I will expect to see you in them on all occasions. I do not want dirt tramping into my carpets, do I, girls?'

'No, Mother.' Veronica and Vivienne replied as one. Their manners, it seemed, were as impeccable as everything about the house.

'Now, your rooms.

Their bedrooms were next to one other at the far end of the landing, as distant as possible from the other members of the family.

Peggy's door was ajar and she pushed it open to find a small window hung with a heavy blackout curtain. A dark-wood chest of drawers and dressing table with a large oval mirror and a jug and bowl stood beneath the window. A wooden towel rail and mahogany wardrobe lined the right-hand wall while a single bed with an ornate metal frame stood to the left. It was considerably larger than Peggy's room at home and was spotlessly tidy.

Judging by Mrs Barnforth's consistently irritated manner, Peggy was unsure whether she should enter or wait to be instructed to do so. The decision was made for her as she was pushed into the room with the single instruction to unpack, the door shut firmly behind her.

Back home in Middlesbrough noise from outside invaded their home, but here the house was silent. Peggy opened the door a crack and peered out, then moved as quietly as possible to Robert's door. The floorboards squeaked beneath her and she froze, but when the sound went unchallenged she opened his door and slipped inside.

The room was smaller with a chest of drawers, a wardrobe and a single bed, by which her brother stood motionless. He looked up as the door opened, his expression hard, his jaw set. He stared at Peggy without speaking and she lowered herself slowly onto the bed where she motioned for her brother to sit alongside her. Robert remained standing. 'She's horrible,' he said. 'I hate her.'

'Shh,' Peggy motioned with her hands for him to keep his voice down. 'You mustn't say that. Mother wouldn't like it.' It was true, mother did not approve of people using hateful words. *There is already far too much badness in the world without others adding to it*, she always said.

Peggy attempted to divert the conversation. 'We'll get used to one another. It's just that she doesn't know us yet. When she sees what a lovely boy you are everything will be different.' Her smile felt strained. 'Come on, let's unpack.' She picked up Robert's brown paper parcel and picked at the knot, remembering the last fingers to tie the knot had been their mother's. Her eyes misted over at the thought and she stroked the string a few times before untying it.

'Right,' she said finally. 'Let's get you settled in.'

They were paraded as the unwelcome guests they were, with everything about them inspected and ridiculed. From Peggy's best Sunday dress and knitted cardigan to Robert's rumpled black shorts, washed-out shirt and tired-looking pullover, nothing met with Mrs Barnforth's high standards. Their carpet slippers only added to the problem, with Peggy's noticeably not her own and Robert's having a frayed hole through which his stocking toes were visible.

While Mother had always done her best to clothe her children, the garments they stood in were the best they owned and Mrs Barnforth looked down upon them with scant regard for their feelings. 'Hand-me-downs,' she sneered. 'That is not something we have need of here, is it girls?'

'No, Mother.' Vivienne and Veronica sniggered, and at that moment Peggy realised there was little possibility they would ever become friends.

house was larger than anything Robert and Peggy had ever been inside before, and Mrs Barnforth was happy to gloat over the fact. Her voice droned on about rules as she led them along the door-line hallway, and as they passed the table holding the lamp and telephone, Robert was mesmerised by its highly-polished surface. He reached out a finger to stroke its polished surface and Mrs Barnforth froze instantly, her face a mask of anger. Her hand struck Robert hard across his cheek, the slap jolting him backwards a step. 'Do not touch anything!' Mrs Barnforth bellowed.

Robert's mouth dropped open, the stinging pain of the slap not making itself felt for a few seconds, its suddenness numbing, and Peggy felt her heart thud as his face finally registered the pain. Robert let out a cry and Peggy folded him into her arms in an attempt to soothe away his anguish, but it was simply too much. For a moment she thought her brother was about to run for the door, but instead, he found space against the wall and pressed himself up against it. His hand cradled his face where he had been struck.

Confrontation had never been Peggy's strong point, in fact she had only ever raised her hand once before in anger, and had paid dearly for it with a beating and hair-pulling from Edith Cass that she had never forgotten. But that had been a childhood argument. This was something entirely different. This was an adult situation, and

17

although she was still a child she knew it was her responsibility to deal with it as an adult. Robert was her responsibility, after all. She had promised their mother.

Peggy felt sure her voice would give away her nerves but she stepped forward nevertheless. 'Our mother would never have struck us like that,' she said. Her voice gained strength through the importance of her words. 'In fact, she would say you must never do that to us again.'

Veronica and Vivienne took a joint intake of breath and the moment seemed to stretch before Peggy like elastic. Had no one dared speak back to Mrs Barnforth before? Certainly, no child had ever shown the courage to do so. Children should be seen and not heard had doubtless never been challenged in this household, but Peggy had said it now, and she felt justified in having done so.

Peggy steeled herself to a slap she felt sure would come and stood her ground on unsteady legs. She was prepared to step out of the way should one come, but Mrs Barnforth seemed taken aback that anyone should dare to speak out. Whether or not she realised her actions had been unnecessarily harsh, any hope that they would not receive further treatment was brushed aside once and for all when Mrs Barnforth leaned forward and hissed, 'Well, young lady, your mother is not here. I am. And from now on you will do *exactly* as I tell you.'

A tin bath stood in front of the kitchen range, the five inches of soapy water allowed by the Home Office as the allocated ration for bathing now growing cold. Peggy and Robert sat at the table in their nightclothes, half a glass of milk and a thinly-cut slice of bread scraped with jam set out before them. Neither had touched it despite their hunger.

Robert looked warily around the kitchen as though expecting to find Mrs Barnforth watching from a corner, then dropped his eyes to stare into his lap. A darkening bruise marked his cheekbone, a vivid reminder of the woman who was to be their replacement mother for the foreseeable future.

'Are you okay?' It was a ridiculous question to ask, but Peggy did not know what else to say.

Robert shook his head, his face angry and sore. He had hardly said a word since sitting down and Peggy nibbled at her supper in the hope it would encourage her brother to do the same. 'I want to go home,' he whispered finally. 'I hate it here.'

Peggy put down her bread and turned to face him. 'Robert, we can't. We have to stay here.' She glanced at the door and dropped her voice further. 'I don't like it either, but... ' She didn't finish the sentence.

Robert sank further into his seat. 'Well I don't care,' he said, a serious tone to his voice. 'I'm running away.'

The words startled Peggy. 'You can't.' she said. 'You don't know where we are for a start, and - '

'Don't care,' Robert said petulantly. 'Anywhere's better than here. She's horrible.' He indicated the door with a flick of his head then dropped his voice further, this time with sorrow rather than the fear of being heard. 'Mother wouldn't have hit me like that.'

He was right, and Peggy put her arm around her brother's shoulders. She tried to appeal to his other self, his rational self, but held out little hope. Once Robert had made his mind up he rarely changed it. 'Please, don't think like that,' she said. 'Give it time. Give *her* time. We just need to get to know each other, that's all. Running away won't change anything, just think how she'll treat us if you end up back here again.'

The prospect of making the situation even worse weighed heavily against the benefits of escape. 'We just have to be clever about everything,' Peggy said. 'Don't give her any opportunity to treat us like that. Remember what mother told us before we left - always be polite, never argue back, and mind your Ps and Qs.'

'But you argued,' said Robert. He looked at Peggy from under a darkened gaze that spoke volumes about his mood.

'I know, and perhaps I shouldn't have, but I did it to protect you, to protect us both. I couldn't let her get away with hitting you like that. It was wrong, so terribly wrong.' Peggy sighed. 'Chances are I've made matters worse, but I do believe it was the right thing to do. In this case, I think Mother would have approved.'

Robert's expression changed at the mention of their Mother and Peggy saw determination in his eyes. He said nothing more and Peggy continued. 'We are guests here and we must be mindful of that. We'll find our place in good time, but we must be patient.'

Robert's expression remained hard. 'I'm going home.'

'Now, Robert Arthur Cotterill, that is the last time I want to hear such words.' Peggy's voice had taken on a firm note. She didn't want to drive a wedge between them, but she loved her brother dearly and needed to put a stop to such an idea. For both their sakes. Peggy raised her eyebrows in what she hoped was a look their mother would use. 'No more of this silly talk, do you hear? It will only make matters worse. We will get through this together, it will simply take a little time.'

Robert shook his head. 'You've got that wrong, sis. I'm not waiting around here to get slapped again.' His expression hardened further and a stony look filled his eyes, a look Peggy had never seen before. 'As soon as I can, I'm off,' he whispered, then leaned closer. 'You coming?

Peggy did not sleep well that first night. She lay awake listening for sounds from next door, but Robert was silent and she was relieved to think he must have fallen asleep. Unless he had slipped out already? She panicked as she contemplated him outside in the darkness, alone and with no idea where to go.

Her mind roamed erratically. How had they come to this? It was certainly not as they had expected, and she felt sure their mother would be horrified to know they were being treated so poorly.

Peggy crept to the window and peered behind the blackout curtain. A thin slither of moonlight was framed between the diagonal tapes that crisscrossed the window. It coloured the darkness with a pale silvery glow, and she imagined it to be their mother keeping vigil as they lay in the darkness. The thought unlocked a few silent tears and gave Peggy reason to consider what their mother would have done to help the situation. She would have tried to speak to Mrs Barnforth and encourage her to understand the children came from a kind family, a loving family where they knew right from wrong. Peggy sighed. If only they could be allowed the opportunity to prove themselves, but a one-sided conversation from downstairs told Peggy any attempt would be a waste of time.

Barnforth did little to conceal her voice as she updated someone by telephone regarding her feelings towards both children. 'Horrid, scruffy children,' she said. 'They are nothing like us, and they will never be part of this family. Never, I tell you.' She laughed sarcastically at something said in reply, then finished with a cut-throat statement that sealed their time with her: 'I advise you to keep a very close eye upon your valuables and make sure everything of worth is locked away. These children are nothing but common street brats, about which there is nothing remotely likeable, and I do not trust them. They came from the gutter, Philippa, and I tell you, that is where they belong.'

Peggy gasped at such an unfair assessment, but Mrs Barnforth had not yet finished. She made an angry sound of agreement with the voice on the other end of the call, then continued. 'And you will do well to keep your girls away from them, as I will do mine, for nothing good will come of their being here. You mark my words.'

Her words cut deeply and Peggy choked at the injustice. She only hoped Robert was asleep and had heard nothing of the conversation, but the sound of his sobbing from the room next door told her differently.

Chapter 2

Mrs Barnforth was nowhere to be seen as they stepped into the kitchen the next morning. They found it to be a large room dominated by a table laden with mixing bowls and a jug of kitchen spoons. Pans of all sizes hung from a wooden frame above the table while a long wooden dresser with all manner of crockery and glassware filled one wall. A kitchen worktop and a stone sink stood on opposite sides of a doorway, while the iron range filled the room with warmth and the aroma of cooking. Robert's stomach rumbled.

An older lady dressed in a dark blue dress with a white pinafore met them as they shuffled through the doorway. She introduced herself as Mrs Woodrow, telling them she cooked and cleaned for Mrs Barnforth.

'Doesn't she do it herself?' asked Robert. 'Mother does.'

'Robert, don't be rude!' The question had taken Peggy by surprise. Hadn't he learnt anything the previous evening?

Their father had always claimed Robert to be 'a bit of a tearaway', and by simply opening his mouth in their current predicament he was sure to bring all sorts of trouble down upon them. Peggy feared she was about to witness that only too soon, but Mrs Woodrow laughed.

'Don't bother yourself, lassie,' she said. 'Lady of house be long gone, and girls don't lower the'selves to eat in here anyways.' She indicated the kitchen. 'That suits me well, mind. I keep kitchen in fine order and don't need those two nosin' round when I'm not 'ere.'

Mrs Woodrow busied herself for a moment with a plate of bacon which was keeping warm atop the kitchen range. 'She were out before you was even awake this mornin', which be usual,' she said. 'Spends most mornings making sure land girls working on her property turn up on time, which she owns most of round 'ere. Seems to think everyone eases off if she not there and don't take kindly to slackers, doesn't our Mrs Barnforth.' Mrs Woodrow fixed them with a firm but not unpleasant stare. 'Round 'ere, most everyone pulls weight for the war effort, as you'll come to realise. Just make sure you do too; she can be a bit of a one can Mrs Barnforth when things don't go 'er way.'

'Now.' Mrs Woodrow turned towards Peggy and Robert with a plate in each hand. 'I been told to only give you one slice o' bread this morning, but by looks, you both need feeding up. Sit the'sen down and let's see how much bacon we can force into you.'

Veronica and Vivienne had left for school without waiting, so Mrs Woodrow showed Robert and Peggy down the hill to a stony path that led across a field towards the village. A few chimney pots and the church spire broke the tree line, below which stood a small gate that led into the schoolyard beyond. Mrs Woodrow watched until the children had stepped through before turning and setting back. It wouldn't do to be missing when Mrs Barnforth returned.

The school was a small building with four sets of windows and a slate-tiled roof topped by a small bell tower. The building had two entrances, one with *Boys* carved into the stone above the door and another with *Girls*. It was much smaller than the school Peggy and Robert had attended back home in Middlesbrough, and as they stepped into the schoolyard they immediately felt eyes upon them.

Some faces were the friends and classmates who had travelled with them yesterday, but most were unfamiliar. Amongst them, Veronica and Vivienne huddled within a group of girls, their whispers and backwards glances enough to inform Peggy and Robert they were the subjects of much unpleasant discussion. Peggy could only hope the other children would be more welcoming.

A group of mothers stood chatting as they waited with younger children for the morning bell to ring. They seemed hesitant to welcome Peggy and Robert - whether because of who they had been billeted with or simply because of their status as wartime evacuees, Peggy did not know - and the atmosphere only added to the feeling of unease. Perhaps none of the mothers dared speak. Perhaps one of them was Philippa, the lady Peggy had overheard Mrs Barnforth speaking to on the telephone the night before, or perhaps the ladies had been relayed the conversation and warned off having anything to do with them. Perhaps Mrs Barnforth's opinion was the law concerning how others were to be viewed, but surely her hold over the villagers could not be so strong? Peggy sighed. *As if being away from home wasn't hard enough.*

Peggy reached out a hand in an attempt to give her brother strength. 'How are you feeling?' she whispered, but Robert did not respond. He shuffled instead towards the schoolyard wall and pressed his back against it. His face held a cold and strained expression and Peggy knew she needed to find something positive to lighten her brother's mood. 'Mrs Woodrow seems nice,' she said at last. 'And you ate plenty.'

Robert's mouth twitched as he thought about the lavish breakfast of bacon and thickly buttered bread. 'She's much nicer than that other cow,' he mumbled. His voice was low with discontent.

'Don't say that,' Peggy chastised. 'It's not nice. Think about what Mother would say.'

Robert gave a quick tilt of the head and twisted his mouth. 'Like she said, Mother's not here. Anyway, I won't be soon either.'

Fear flooded through Peggy like ice water. 'Now that's enough of that kind of talk. We have to stay here and – '

A familiar voice called Robert's name and they both turned. Alfred Hitchins bounded towards them, his face full of smiles and excitement. His clothes were cleaner than the last time they had seen him, having been washed, and he wore a pair of shoes that had not been his on the journey out. He had also bathed, which in truth was a rarity and a necessity for poor Alfred, and this morning he smelled strongly of carbolic soap. He launched straight into a barrage of information and questions without offering Robert and Peggy the opportunity to pass comment or ask anything: *Who are you staying with? I'm staying with Mr and Mrs Wilson and they're really nice and let me have a bath and something to eat before I went to bed last night. I've got my own room. Have you got your own room? Mine is really big with a wardrobe and a nightstand and a fluffy bedspread, even though I don't like fluffy things, and we have a dog called Charlie and a cat called Petunia or Petty for short –*

Alfred was wrapped up in his new life, desperate to share every detail, and after a brief pause for breath, a fresh round of unstoppable information ensued. He was halfway through another explanation when Mary and Frederick Barnaby took over the conversation. 'Who picked you up last night?' Mary's query was edged with a more searching question, and when Peggy's short answer of Mrs Barnforth did not go deep enough for her liking, she glanced sideways at Robert. 'But what is she like? I mean, is she nice?' It appeared word had already spread between the evacuees.

'She hit me,' Robert growled. Last evening's events were still very much on his mind. 'And she shouted,' he added.

'She hit you?' Mary was shocked. 'That's terrible!'

Peggy turned her brother's face towards Mary with a finger and Mary and Fred moved in to look at the bruise. 'She did that? She really hit you?'

Robert nodded.

'Why? What did you do?'

'Touched a table,' said Robert.

'Was that all?'

Robert nodded. There was nothing more to say on the matter and no time as a man dressed in a dark suit and tie stepped onto the schoolyard. He rang a bell and the press of bodies swept the girls towards one doorway, the boys towards another. Peggy hung back. She had no desire to be separated from her brother with little warning.

A tall lady wearing a green gabardine dress and her hair in a bun introduced herself as Miss Fenwick. After a brief chat, she led them first to the girls' corridor where Peggy hung her coat, and then to the boys'. From there she led them into a classroom. 'Now you sit here,' said Miss Fenwick to Robert, indicating a seat next to a tall lad Robert would come to know as Will Atkins. She took Peggy to an end seat four rows from the back. 'This is Maude, Will's sister.' She spoke directly to the girl, her intent clear. 'Maude will look after you, now won't you Maude?'

Maude shuffled in her seat, uncomfortable at being put on the spot, but nodded and mumbled in agreement.

When Miss Fenwick had gone, Maude moved along the bench to allow Peggy to slide on next to her. She seemed nervous meeting someone new but it was a vulnerability Peggy shared, and within minutes something told the girls they would soon become the best of friends.

Peggy spent morning break skipping with Maude Atkins and Fay Dunbar, while the local boys were eager to hear everything about bombs and air raids and crashed

German aircraft from Robert and the other evacuees. Between them, what they didn't know they made up, but Robert was less talkative than the others. He stood on the fringes of the conversation, and it wasn't until one of the boys mentioned Robert had the compass needle from a downed German bomber that he found himself the centre of attention.

A circle closed quickly around Robert and with a little encouragement he pulled the needle from his pocket. It was white with a red tip, about two inches long and cut to a point at one end. A round hole and a small slot marked the pivot point where the needle had been pinned upon the compass face. The needle had a slight curve along its length as though it had been torn free in an impact.

'Whoa! Where did the get tha?' Archie Summers was a farmer's son, his countryside accent so strong with local sounds, at times he was difficult to understand. He was eager to hold the needle, but Robert wasn't keen to relinquish possession.

'My father found it,' Robert said. 'He saw the plane come down and found it in the wreckage.' He gripped the needle tightly; it was the last thing his father had given him when his leave ended and it was a very special keepsake. *A compass to guide you*, his father had told him.

'Is 'e pilot? Did 'e shoot it dahn?' Archie was enthralled by the tale. The other local boys made agreeable noises of interest and nodded at the importance of the question.

Robert shook his head. 'He's no pilot. Does top-secret stuff though. Can't tell you what cos I don't rightly know myself.' That was what his dad had told him, and his father being involved in such important work made being apart more bearable. Heads nodded again in understanding and a chorus of *Oohs* and *Aahs* followed, and for the first time since leaving home yesterday, Robert felt included.

A hand made a sudden grab for the needle and Robert pulled it back, but the invading fingers remained clamped to the pointed end and Robert felt it twist in his grip.

'Gee it 'ere! Let's 'av a look!' said a voice.

'Get off!' Robert nipped the needle tightly and pulled it towards him. He found himself face to face with Harry Grenton, who at a head taller than Robert looked down on him, but Robert didn't care. It was his keepsake and nobody was taking it from him.

'Ah said, gee it 'ere!' Harry Grenton pulled on it one more time but Robert was not about to give it up, and that was when he bloodied Harry Grenton's nose with an upward right. It was a single blow, just as his father had taught him, and it did the trick.

Harry Grenton released his grip and backed up. He put his hand to his nose, saw blood and sat down hard. All eyes were suddenly on him, then back on Robert. Peggy realised what Robert had done and her mind raced from the scene before her to what their Mother would say, and then to thoughts of Mrs Barnforth. Her knees went weak.

Everything went silent until a single laugh filled the schoolyard.

It was Veronica Barnforth.

The walk home was slow, partly because it was uphill all the way, but mostly because neither Peggy nor Robert wanted to return to Mrs Barnforth's too soon. Peggy didn't let on, but she had a feeling Mrs Barnforth would already know about her brother's run-in with Harry Grenton.

Robert drew an unsteady line in the mud with a stick as he and Will strolled uphill. Their voices were peppered with laughter and boyish silliness while the girls talked about their own lives.

Maude told Peggy stories about growing up close to the sea, how she had liked to play on the sand dunes and pick shells from the beach, but it was fenced off now with barbed wire and nobody was allowed down. She talked about living on a farm, how it was her job to feed the chickens and collect eggs from the coop before school and after, and of the time she didn't lock the gate properly and a fox had snuck in and killed all their chickens during the night.

The more Maude talked, the more Peggy realised how different their lives were, yet at the same time they had so much in common. Maude had only been out of the village on a few occasions to Sandsend, Runswick Bay and Staithes, and down into Whitby to buy fish. Peggy hadn't been further from home than Linthorpe and Acklam, and to North Ormesby for the weekly market, so although they had grown up in totally different places, with entirely different experiences, they had more in common than either of them realised.

They stopped at the gate to Ravenscroft House, Peggy and Robert's home for the foreseeable future. The track to the house opened onto a cobbled farmyard with the outbuildings they had sensed in the darkness the night before. The horse that had greeted them on their arrival now watched them from behind a low fence. *Listening*, thought Peggy, as if she didn't know better.

Better go,' said Maude. 'Mother gets cross if we be late from school. Says she's enough to do lookin' after farm wi'out doing our jobs too.'

Peggy nodded, but as Maude turned she asked, 'Is your father away too?' By away, she meant was he fighting the Germans.

Maude nodded, but Will answered for them both. 'We've had letters an he's been back once, but Mother finds it difficult doin' all. Barnforth owns farm but don't care father is away. Land girls work fields every day, but she ain't bothered how hard it be for us. Don't much care either. When she comes to farm, she's just 'orrible.'

From what Peggy had witnessed the previous night, Will's description of Mrs Barnforth seemed about right.

Maude glanced around in case Veronica and Vivienne had crept up on them to listen, but only the horse showed any interest. 'Most round about calls her Bolshy Barnsforth.' She giggled. 'Watch she don't hear you though. Can't say she'd much like it.'

grinned, amused by the rudeness of it all and glad Robert appeared not to have heard what Maude had told them. She dreaded to think what would be said once they made it indoors, and having a comment such as *Bolshy Barnforth* up his sleeve wasn't something she was comfortable for him to have.

Chapter 3

Mrs Barnforth was waiting for them while Veronica and Vivienne watched from a doorway. Peggy could see by the smirk on their faces they had been waiting for this moment, their story already told.

'...and that is *precisely* the reason I was unwilling to take you two – ' Mrs Barnforth pointed at them both as she searched for the right description. ' – you two miscreants under my roof! I warned them something like this would happen. I warned them that bringing children like *you* into our village, into our *homes*, was a mistake of the highest order!' She spluttered in disbelief.

Neither Peggy nor Robert knew what a miscreant was, but it was of no concern; the barely controlled simmer of anger that flowed from Mrs Barnforth was enough to assure them it was not good.

Peggy stepped closer to her brother, his body tense, his eyes large at the tirade of abuse Mrs Barnforth threw at them both, and she sensed his emotions were hidden just beneath the surface. She could only hope his true feelings did not come tumbling out. Robert had a blazing temper when riled and Peggy hugged him, sharing in his anger at their treatment and desperate to give him the strength to hold himself in check. How could she say such things? How could Mrs Barnforth be so rude, so... Maude's words came back to her... *so horrible?* Peggy's inner core shook and she tried to swallow, but her tongue caught in her mouth and she coughed, anger bubbling up in defense of her brother.

Despite her fear, Peggy decided this was the time to try and reason with Mrs Barnforth. It was what her mother would have done, and she took strength from that knowledge. 'Mrs Barnforth – ' Peggy began, her voice little more than a croak, but she was cut off as though she hadn't been heard. Veronica or Vivienne giggled. Peggy did not know which of the girls it was, and she didn't much care.

'How *dare* you taint the name and reputation of this family with such behaviour! To think my girls have been associated with such...' Mrs Barnforth stumbled for words again. Her mouth opened and closed soundlessly as she physically trembled with rage, '...such common, low-life...'

Mrs Barnforth was unable to finish. Instead, she thrust out a hand. 'Give me the pointer, the needle, the...' she spluttered again, '...whatever it is!'

Robert's hand faltered. He had always been taught to be respectful, and for a moment it looked as though he was about to do as Mrs Barnforth had instructed him, and then he found his resolve and shoved his hand deep into his pocket. The needle felt smooth and slim in his fingers and he gripped it tightly. It gave him strength. His father's strength.

'No.' Robert's voice was small but firm. There was no indication of the emotion he was feeling.

'What did you say?' Mrs Barnforth spoke slowly, her voice a tone lower. Veronica and Vivienne's eyes widened and they took an uncomfortable step backwards. This situation wasn't turning out how Peggy wanted it to and she suddenly felt very uncomfortable. She dreaded what was to come next.

'I said no.' Robert seemed to find further strength after his first denial. Peggy swallowed hard.

Mrs Barnforth took a step closer. 'Say that again, child, and I swear I will –

Peggy's chest swelled with defiance at the prospect of violence once more towards her brother. She would later have no idea where the courage came from but would deem it the right thing to have done. 'I won't allow you to hit my brother again,' she said firmly. Despite her worries, she was prepared to stand her ground for both of them. She had promised their Mother. Mrs Barnforth was certainly no stranger to dishing out justice to those who crossed her, but the words left Peggy's mouth before she even realised she had said them. Her voice sounded weak to her own ears and she swallowed hard, but she stood there for her brother. With her brother.

Mrs Barnforth glared coldly but did not challenge the girl's stand. She turned slowly towards Robert instead. 'Give. Me. The. Needle.' She thrust her hand out once again and Robert refused. Peggy felt a change in the atmosphere and it concerned her greatly, the air noticeably cooler in the confines of the hallway, and she steeled herself to step forward, to place herself in danger if Mrs Barnforth raised a hand once more against her brother. Instead, Mrs Barnforth grabbed Robert by the wrist.

Robert was not expecting such a move. Nor was Peggy. His hand came free from his pocket more easily than expected, the needle visibly stuck within his fist, and Mrs Barnforth dragged it towards her. She snatched at it with her other hand and attempted to prise his fingers open.

'Ow!' Robert twisted his arm in an attempt to keep the needle from her grasp. 'Gerroff!' he yelled. 'It's mine!'

'Give. It. Here!'

Peggy froze in stunned disbelief as Mrs Barnforth gripped her brother's wrist. He squealed as hot pain stabbed up his arm and he twisted again to free himself, but Mrs Barnforth dug her fingers into his palm, grabbed at the end of the needle and pulled.

'No! It's mine! You can't - '

With a final flick of her wrist, the needle slid free from Robert's fingers. He grabbed at it with his other hand but wasn't quick enough, and Mrs Barnforth stepped back, a look of satisfaction on her face.

Robert lunged after it. 'Give it back!'

Mrs Barnforth lifted the needle out of his reach and looked at it quizzically. 'And this is what you were fighting about?' She turned it over and peered at both sides.

Robert grabbed at Mrs Barnforth's elbow. He pulled it downwards and the needle was suddenly within reach. 'Argh! Give it back!' he yelled. He grabbed for it once more but Mrs Barnforth switched the needle to her other hand and Robert was left grasping at empty air. He threw his full weight upwards and dragged her elbow towards him.

'Take your hands off me, child! Who do you think – '

Robert's emotions got the better of him and his eyes filled with tears as he pulled hard on the elbow. He jumped at the needle in desperation but Mrs Barnforth whipped it from his grasp once more.

Everything happened so quickly. Peggy found herself unable to intervene but knew she had to do something, and now was the moment. She stepped forwards, hoping to disarm the situation. 'Please give it back,' she said in a calm and appealing voice, her hand out, palm upwards. 'Father gave him that. It was the last thing he did before he went back to war. It's Robert's special treasure. His keepsake.'

'This?' Mrs Barnforth glanced at it again. 'And what, pray, is it a needle from?'

Robert didn't step back. He remained in grasping distance should the opportunity present itself. 'A German bomber,' he said, his voice thick, his eyes reddened by the onset of tears. 'Father found it for me.' His voice was desperate, angry and upset. All he wanted was the needle back.

'A bomber?' Mrs Barnforth turned her nose up. 'A *German* bomber? In *my* house?' She fixed Robert with an angry stare. 'Oh, no. I do not think so. Not in this house. Don't you think the Germans have caused enough trouble without bringing a piece of them into my home?' She looked at the needle once more, disgust etched upon her face, and then at Robert. 'A *German* bomber?' she repeated.

'Please,' said Robert. He was on the verge of hysterics, his hand held out in despair. *This needle means we'll always find our way to one another*, his father had told him, his hand atop his son's as he spoke. *Keep it with you, keep it close and I'll never be far. I promise.* It was a belief Robert had held onto since that day, a belief that was more important than anything. To lose the needle now would be like striking him through his heart.

Mrs Barnforth knew nothing of the needle's importance, and nor would she have cared even if she did. She shook her head in response to Robert's plea, seeming to enjoy the torment. 'No. Most certainly not,' she said, and with that, she twisted the needle around on itself, folded it in two and twisted it again to make a ball.

Robert's face crumpled in disbelief, his tears of anguish and distress filling the room. 'My needle!' he shrieked. 'My needle!' He jumped in an attempt to grab the crumpled remains, but Mrs Barnforth held it out of reach.

Desperate to retrieve the special link with his father and take back what was rightfully his, Robert kicked out at Mrs Barnforth. He struck her hard in both shins and drew his foot back ready to repeat the action. 'I wish we'd never been sent here!' he yelled. 'I wish we'd never left home and I wish I'd never met you! You're horrible!' he finished, and then he kicked out again, his shoe catching her squarely in both shins a second time, causing Mrs Barnforth to wince as a blossom of pain stabbed at her legs. Veronica and Vivienne cried out in fright and rushed forward to help their mother, but she shrugged them off. They stood behind her, shock upon their faces and tears in their eyes as they waited to see what would happen next.

Robert's response was wrong, Peggy knew, and she should have stepped in and apologised and tried to put things right. Their mother would have been mortified at Robert's actions and would have expected nothing less from Peggy than to try and calm the situation, but she could not find it in herself to show sympathy for Mrs Barnforth, or remorse for her brother's actions. After the way Mrs Barnforth had treated them both since arriving yesterday, after witnessing the despicable actions displayed towards her brother, his feelings and their situation, somehow Peggy could not blame him. Yes, it was wrong. Yes, it was disrespectful, but she knew why he had reacted the way he had.

'Why, you little devil!' Mrs Barnforth bent over and cupped her shins in both hands. Robert's kicks had been painful, the skin red and already bruising, and she was eager for them not to be repeated. She pushed Robert away as she tried to regain her composure, and suddenly their faces were on the same level. 'Get out of my house!' she hissed directly into Robert's face. 'Get out now and don't come back!' She straightened up and threw the remains of the needle onto the carpet as though a parting gift. 'Ever!'

Robert stepped back, his face full of anger and tears, his world no longer between the safe pace he needed to be and the place he wanted to be. His body was wracked with sobs so deep that he struggled to breathe, and Peggy thought for a moment he was going to collapse. Then he grabbed the screwed-up remains of the needle, looked at his sister, and bolted from the house.

Robert ran blindly. Tears filled his eyes until he could barely see, but still he ran on. His breath was ragged and his chest hurt as he ran across fields of mud and through long grass that grasped at his legs. He fell several times but picked himself up, although he had no idea where he was or where he might end up, and he did not care. He just ran, his only plan being to get as far away from Mrs Barnforth, as far away from everyone, as he could.

He found himself running towards a patch of forest that sat on a rise above the village, its position prominent yet isolated. The trees were all but motionless in the late afternoon sun, their low-hanging boughs dark and heavy, their shadows secretive, and he felt drawn towards them as though he would be safe there.

Throwing himself down against the dry stone wall surrounding the woodland, he sat to regain his breath. He wiped at his eyes as voices filled his head, the horrible things Mrs Barnforth had said still ringing in his ears, the things she had done still in his head, and he thought of his sister. He knew she would be worried about him and didn't want her to be in trouble because of what he had done, but he couldn't bear to be anywhere near Mrs Barnforth.

His mind was made up. He would run away as he had said. He would run all the way home if he had to because he couldn't stay here any longer. Once he told their mother what had happened she would come and take Peggy back and they would all be together again. Yes, that was it. His decision was made.

And with that, Robert climbed over the wall and stepped down into the seclusion of the forest.

Peggy raced outside after her brother, her throat too tight and choked for her shouts to be heard. She heard the door slam behind her and realised Mrs Barnforth had locked her out, but that hardly mattered. If Robert had run away at home she would have known where to look for him, but here, in the countryside where he didn't know anyone or where he was, he would quickly find himself lost. A wave of sickness rose in her throat and she set off at a run.

She followed her brother along the farm track opposite, but the field was large and Robert soon shrank into the distance. He had always been a much faster runner, despite his smaller size, and she struggled to keep up. He was soon out of sight.

Tears welled once again behind her eyes, more from panic this time than the emotions of earlier, and Peggy stopped at a gate to wipe her eyes and look around. She gripped onto its weathered timber, its splinters sharp under her fingers, and the sensation brought reality to the moment. Robert was nowhere to be seen.

The world blurred behind hot tears and fresh panic tightened her chest. 'Oh, Robert, where are you?' she whispered. 'Where are you?'

Peggy searched for what seemed like hours. *He can't stay out all night*, she thought, *but where will he go?* She found herself talking to the open countryside, looking for answers where there were none, and then saw footprints in the mud. They appeared about her brother's size. Surely they had to be his?

The track dried up as she followed it. She began to fear she might lose the footsteps altogether, but then the path forked left towards a forest that grew atop a gentle rise while a cluster of buildings nestled upon the level ground to the right.

Which way? The tracks vanished suddenly and she was left with a decision: take the path left towards the forest or right towards the buildings? *He must have taken one of the paths, but if I make the wrong choice I'll never find him!*

No, Peggy told herself, not the forest. *He doesn't like the dark. He would choose the houses,* and with that, she started down the track towards the place she prayed he would be.

*   *   *

Robert stepped down nervously into the wood. The shadows were cool and restful, and he felt his emotions begin to settle. A large raven, its beak and feathers as black as coal, fluttered about in the upper branches as Robert worked his way along a track. It flew from branch to branch, watching him with intelligent eyes that missed nothing.

The more steps he took, the more he noticed the appearance of the trees, the lines and swirls in their bark making it appear as though faces watched his every move. He swallowed hard, his knees suddenly weak, and he felt a desperate need to see daylight once more. He gripped the remains of the needle, its presence reassuring within his fingers, and he made a silent plea to it for help as he moved deeper into the wood. Somehow he hoped his father would help him, would lead him to safety, and he stumbled upon a fork in the path where he felt compelled to turn right.

Each step became faster than the one before, his toe catching his heel at one point and causing him to stumble, but he regained his balance and rushed on until he was running. All the while he had a sense of the woodland moving, keeping pace with him, its sounds carrying from tree to tree as though a whispered conversation was being held behind his back. But the trees couldn't really be moving. They couldn't really be talking. Could they?

Robert clambered over the wall and raced downhill. When he was far enough away to feel safe he lay in the long grass, the screwed-up needle still clamped between his fingers, and he gave a silent thanks to his father while his heart slowed. The grass under his body was a relief and he relished its softness, yet the feeling of being watched remained.

Using the long grass as cover he looked around. The forest seemed far away now and he eyed it suspiciously, the need to put some distance between himself and that place overwhelming. He was desperate to start moving again but had no idea where he was or even from which way he had come. The sky had begun to turn orange in places and he realised he had been in the wood longer than he thought.

Climbing to his knees, Robert decided to follow the field downhill towards a low point where the sea cut a straight line across the horizon. He had never seen the ocean before and it sparkled in the setting sun, its shimmer creating a sense of calm, and he felt a growing urge to go there.

He set off at a steady pace but did not see the dark figure watching him from the edge of the forest. To anyone observing, Carrion was but a strange old man who lived on the hilltops, yet his history went far deeper than anyone understood, his purpose more meaningful than history remembered, and despite his advanced years, his attention remained sharp, his eyes focused upon the smallest of details.

With the aid of his beloved ravens, Carrion missed nothing, and he watched the departing figure of the boy with great interest.

Chapter 4

The hamlet was composed of three small cottages separated by low wooden fences, their side gardens filled with rows of carefully tended vegetables. The cottages opened directly onto a track to the front, and as she approached, Peggy saw the door to the first cottage was open.

A lad a few years older sat on the doorstep, and as she approached he looked up. Not recognising her, he asked, 'Can I 'elp you, lass?'

Peggy was glad at not having to knock. The thought made her nervous, and she felt worried enough already.

'I'm looking for my brother,' she said. 'He's run away.' She glanced around as she spoke and indicated the unknown landscape. 'He has no idea where he is.'

The lad looked confused 'Run away? From where?'

Peggy had no desire to admit it was from Mrs Barnforth, so she mentioned where they were staying instead. 'We've been put up at Ravenscroft House. We're evacuees,' she finished, although she thought it likely her clothes and accent gave the truth away anyway.

The lad nodded. 'You're living wi' Barnforth?' Peggy nodded and he shook his head. 'Feel sorry for you.' He turned and shouted back into the cottage. 'Ma! Maude's friend be here!'Peggy was confused. Did he know all about them already?

A woman in dungarees and a checked shirt leaned out over the doorstep. She wiped her hands on a towel, her dark curly hair held back by a flowered headscarf. 'You be Maude's friend from school?' she asked.

Peggy nodded, and before she could say more, tears filled her eyes. She tried to speak, but her voice was little more than a croak. 'Hey, what be the matter?' The lady stepped down from the doorstep and put an arm across Peggy's shoulders.

Peggy choked back the tears enough to manage a reply. 'It's my brother. He's missing. He ran away and I don't know where he is.' A fresh bout of tears overtook her and the lady hugged her close.

'So that be Robert? Will's friend from today?' Peggy nodded and the lady continued. 'Well, let's see what we can do, shall we?' she said. 'You best come in. I'm Mrs Atkins, Maude's Ma,' she said kindly, 'but you best call me Betty like most do.' She shepherded Peggy towards the door and motioned the boy on the doorstep into action. 'Phillip, go tell others they 'ave visitor.'

The kitchen was small. A table and four chairs filled the middle of the stone floor while a black kitchen range stood against one wall and a stone sink below the window opposite. A kitchen dresser with shelves and a few pots and ornaments filled the wall by an open pantry door, while a wooden clothes airer hung suspended from the ceiling. Socks and shirts were draped over its wooden spars like sleeping bodies.

'Sit yoursen down, lass.' Betty pulled a chair up opposite and sat facing Peggy, Phillip on the far side of the table. 'Now, tell all,' Betty said.

Maude rushed into the kitchen, her nightclothes dishevelled from sleep. 'Peggy!' she cried.

Will stood in the doorway. 'Where's Robert?'

'Lassie were just about to tell,' said Betty, 'so sit down and hush, there's a good lad.'

Once Peggy began speaking everything tumbled out, from the way they had been treated the previous night to Robert's fight at school, and finally what had happened on their return home. She finished with Robert running off and her losing him in the fields. As she spoke, Peggy felt drawn in by the appearance of the woman opposite. It was like sitting opposite their mother.

Betty sat back, visibly upset at everything she had heard. 'Well, that be no way to treat you, that be for sure,' she said. 'But then, that be Mrs Barnforth for you. Never were one to lavish much attention on anyone but her own. Nasty piece of work, that one,' she said. 'Can't believe Gov'ment put you two wi' her.' She shook her head. 'Should never 'ave 'appened.'

Maude edged onto the chair alongside Peggy and linked arms. Her voice sounded weak when she next spoke. 'What are we going to do?'

'I'll go along track by woods and circle back to coastal path.' Will spoke before his mother had a chance to offer her thoughts, a plan already set in his mind. 'You go other way wi' Maude and Peggy. Phillip can come wi' us, and we'll take Edith from next door. There be plenty to look, so don't worry,' he added, his words upbeat, his confidence strong.

Betty nodded and placed her hand on Peggy's. 'We'll find your brother,' she said. 'There be few paths round 'ere. Unless he cut across open fields, he'll come by this way int end.'

As they stepped out of the kitchen Betty pulled Will to one side. 'It be gettin' dark soon, so mind you steer clear o' woods,' she whispered. 'And watch out for Carrion.'

*   *   *

Robert stood on the cliffs overlooking the ocean. He had heard people talk as though it went on forever, and although he had seen pictures he would never have believed it until now. His father had taken him down to the edge of River

Tees.a few times, but that was a trickle compared to what lay before him.

The sun lay upon the horizon, its light blinding, the sea golden with the last rays of its reflected glow. He watched as waves rolled onto the beach below and a flutter of excitement somersaulted in the pit of his stomach at their sound. He wanted to take the steps down from the coastal path and walk on the sand, but daylight was waning, and his path was blocked by coils of barbed wire and a sign which read:

BEACH CLOSED

NO PUBLIC ACCESS

BY ORDER OF THE MINISTRY OF DEFENCE

In truth, the beach was little more than a small cove, but like Whitby's beaches further down the coast, it was strung with coils of barbed wire to make it difficult for invading troops if the enemy did try to come ashore.

Robert stood a while longer. It took all his willpower to drag himself away from the view, and when he finally turned back to the path he scooped a handful of windblown sand and allowed it to trickle through his fingers. It was fine and silky, yet cool despite the heat of the day.

A thin plume of smoke rose beyond the dunes and he reasoned it must belong to a nearby cottage. He considered his next move - he couldn't go back to Mrs Barnforth's house, in fact, he had *no* intention of going back there – but what if he continued towards the source of the smoke and there was no one to help him? Or there was, and they took him back to Mrs Barnforth? No, that wasn't an option, so what else could he do? He could sleep outside, maybe find a barn or a shed, but what if it rained or was cold? And what about Peggy? He felt a tightness in his chest as he thought about the way Mrs Barnforth must be treating her after what he had done, but his mind was made up. Perhaps he could find somewhere to sleep for the night and go back for her in the morning? They could grab their belongings and run home together. Peggy would know best how to do that.

A distant voice caught his attention, and as it grew closer he looked around. Where was there to hide? The path dropped away to the dunes to one side but the barbed wire would stop him from going further, and on the opposite side of the track there was nothing but open grassland. He supposed he could try and hide amongst the grasses, find a low spot, but there didn't seem any possibility of laying out of sight. And then there was the question of what he would say to anyone who queried what he was doing. He couldn't very well say he was running away.

Three figures came into view around a curve in the path and Robert backed up to keep himself out of sight. The path straightened behind him and the figures rounded the curve once more, their voices thick with local accents, and then another voice joined in. A different voice. A familiar voice.

Before he had the opportunity to react Peggy launched herself along the path towards him. 'Robert! Robert! Where have you been?'

Peggy flung herself at her brother. She almost knocked him off his feet and he struggled to remain upright. 'Get off!' he groaned, his complaining all for show.

A lady approached. For an instant, Robert was concerned it was Mrs Barnforth, but when she knelt before him her face and words were friendly and he was relieved to see it was someone else. 'Hello there. You be Robert? We been lookin' for you. I'm Betty Atkins, Will an' Maude's mother.' She took hold of Peggy's hand. 'Children been worried sick about you. So have we all, if truth be known.' She looked at him closely. 'Is the 'urt?'

Robert shook his head and glanced at his sister, his eyes wary. He didn't want to give too much away in case it put him in more trouble.

'Well, we're glad to 'ave found you, but we need to make way inside. Light goes quickly round 'ere so we best get back. We can decide what to do after.'

Robert took a defensive step backwards. 'I'm not going back! Not ever! Not the way she treats us. I'll run home from here if I have to - don't want to be here anyway!' He glanced at his sister. 'Mother'll have us back. She won't let us stay here when we tell her what - '

Peggy took hold of her brother's arm. 'No, Robert. Betty doesn't mean back there. Maude doesn't live far. We'll go there tonight. Betty won't let anything bad happen to us, will you Betty?'

'Where did you go?'

Robert sat between Will and his sister. Peggy hoped he would open up but he just shrugged. He still had a look of unease about him, but that seemed hardly surprising. 'You're too quick a runner for me,' said Peggy. 'I lost you. I couldn't keep up. Didn't you hear me shouting?'

His eyes downcast, Robert shook his head. He pulled the twisted remains of the needle from his pocket and sat with it in cupped hands. Peggy felt her emotions well up, the impact of what Mrs Barnforth had done striking her afresh. Finally, Robert spoke. 'Why did she do that?' he said. 'It was nasty. Mother wouldn't have done it.'

'I know, and I'm sorry,' Peggy said, as though it had all been her fault.

Robert suddenly looked small and lost, as though he could crawl up into a ball and stay that way. 'I'm sorry I left you,' he said. His eyes moistened and he wiped them with his sleeve.

'It were a mean thing to do,' said Betty, then added, 'but mean be what that woman is. Not a good bone in 'er body, that one.' She shuffled uncomfortably, unsure she should have spoken such a sentiment aloud. What if Robert or Peggy repeated it and Mrs Barnforth heard? 'I think it best you not repeat that,' she said. 'She don't have good word for me at best o' times.'

'So where did you go?' asked Will.

Robert shrugged. 'Don't know. I just ran, ended up in some woods. Won't go there again, though. It was creepy. Scared me.'

'Carrion's Wood, up ont hill?' Will sucked air through his teeth, the atmosphere in the small kitchen suddenly heavy. All eyes were on Robert and he suddenly looked worried.

'Why?' he said. 'Was that bad?'

Betty Atkins' voice was small and timid, as though speaking the name was a terrible deed in itself. 'No one ever ventures into Carrion's Wood. Best you don't again, if you wants my advice.'

Peggy glanced at the faces around the table, everyone seemingly alarmed by the name spoken aloud, but not prepared to explain further. 'Why not?'

Phillip had remained silent until then, but his voice was cautious when he spoke. 'That place be off-limits round 'ere,' he said. 'All village knows it and no one ever goes in.' He dropped his voice further. 'There be strange goings-on up there. Strange noises too, 'specially after dark.'

'What's in there?' Robert asked. He looked worried. 'Is it haunted?'

'Not haunted,' said Phillip, but he paused, looking for the right words. 'But it do seem wood be alive in some way.'

Phillip cast a glance at his Mother. Her expression told him he had said enough and she reached out a hand to Robert. 'Now don't you be worrying,' said Betty. 'Just promise me you won't be going up there again.'

'What do you mean, alive?' said Robert, Betty's request going unheard. Something in his voice told them he had good reason to ask.

Phillip avoided his mother's warning gaze. 'Let's just say wood has 'abit o' changin'. It look different one day to next, then no change for weeks or months. Like I say, it be alive somehow.'

Robert opened his mouth to speak and then thought better of it. Will spoke instead. 'What did the see in there?'

Despite the summer warmth, Robert felt oddly cool. He shoved his hands between his knees, the needle still wrapped inside his fist. He paled visibly as he remembered where he had been only a short time before, how it felt as though the trees were moving around him, whispering between themselves, watching him. 'I...' he began, but the words to finish his thought eluded him. Finally, he found his voice. 'I felt the trees were watching me,' he said. 'It was like they had faces. It was like they were moving.'

'That be just a figment o' your mind,' said Betty. She felt the need to lighten the moment but wasn't sure she had succeeded. Too much had been said already.

'And if you see Carrion, stay clear,' Phillip said, repeating what Betty had instructed earlier. 'I won't speak wi' 'im. Nobody will.'

Robert looked alarmed. Peggy shuffled in her seat. 'Who's Carrion?' he asked.

Betty waved a settle-down hand at her son, the conversation having passed the point she thought appropriate. They still had to sort out what to do with Peggy and Robert before the hour got too late. 'Carrion be a strange old man who lives int wood. Bit of a hermit really,' she said. 'No one knows how long he's lived there. If you ask anyone int village, nobody would know a time before he were there. And I'm going back hundreds o' years, mind you. All round here call him Carrion for he always has ravens about him. Big, horrible, noisy squawkers they be, but take my word for it, you best just steer clear if you cross paths wi' him.'

'Hundred's of years?' asked Peggy. 'But nobody lives that long.'

'That may be,' said Betty, 'but he's always been there. Never comes into village and don't make bother for others, but cross his path too closely and he'll send you on your way. Just steer clear and you won't go far wrong.'

'Is that why it's called Carrion's Wood?' Robert wondered if it had been Carrion watching him instead of the trees. It seemed a more sensible idea.

Betty shrugged. 'Folk round here call it that on account o' birds and his always bein' there, but wood is believed to belong to family o' Raven the Righteous. Legend has it he were a knight born o' these parts over thousand years ago. Whether Carrion be descendent, no one knows. Whether land belongs to him, no one rightly know either. It all just hear-say really.'

She stood up and drew the blackout curtain over the kitchen window and lit the oil lantern on the table before them, more for something to do than something needed. It cast a warm light and softened the atmosphere, filling the silence between them. 'And now to you,' she said.

That was Betty's way of changing the subject. She faced Robert and Peggy and an uncomfortable smile creased her mouth as she sat forward. She wrung her hands subconsciously. 'What 'appened wi' Mrs Barnforth were terrible, and having that done to a treasure your father give you were unforgivable, but you be under Mrs Barnforth's care and I can't interfere. If it were up to me you could stay 'ere tonight and we'd sort everythin' int mornin', but I daren't cross 'er.'

Robert wasn't listening. 'Please don't send me back.   I don't want to go.'

'She doesn't want us,' added Peggy. Tears of pain at being ripped from home and thrust into a world neither of them knew was painful enough, but the pain of being unwanted was simply too much to bear.

'Mum, please,' Maude spoke through tears of her own. 'Peggy can sleep wi' me, Robert wi' Will. We can do that. Honest, we can.'

Will nodded. 'That be right wi' me.'

Maude wrapped her arms around her mother and hugged her. She may have only met Peggy and Robert that morning, but already she felt for her friends and couldn't bear to think what life was like with Mrs Barnforth. 'Please, mother,' she whispered. 'Please.'

Torn by the need to help, but tied by the children being billeted with Mrs Barnforth, Betty knew the matter was out of her hands. Rules and legal red tape no doubt bound the children to their host, not to mention the fact that Mrs Barnforth was her employer. If she lost her job because of this, Mrs Barnforth would take the greatest of pleasure in evicting them from their home and they would find themselves homeless.

Betty sagged into her chair, the weight of emotion bearing down until she felt worn and useless. She watched the fear in the children's eyes, the pain of rejection and their desperate need to be somewhere safe all the proof she needed that something had to change.

Sending them back would be cruel and heartless, and her maternal instincts told her she must do whatever was necessary to protect the children from such a fate.

Betty realised she had no choice.

The walk along the track was familiar. Even in the dark, Betty knew every dip and turn, but each step felt like a punch to the stomach. The last thing she had wanted this evening was the walk to knock on her employer's door and inform her the children would not be home before tomorrow, but she had little choice and had left the children tucked up in bed, topping and tailing with one another as many families had taken to doing where space was tight.

Betty approached the end of the track. She crossed the road on unwilling legs and walked down the short driveway into the farmyard, the windows of Ravenscroft House dark, the blackout curtains pulled across to block any escaping light and render the house invisible to German aircraft. Only the crescent moon cast any light, but it was little more than a glimmer, leaving the front of the house in shadow.

She stood back from the doorstep and steeled herself for the conversation to come. *Good evening, Mrs Barnforth. Sorry to disturb you at such late hour, but I felt it duty to come and inform you children be safe in my 'ome. They be too upset to return right now, but be assured they goin' to school tomorrow.* She felt compelled to add *and will return to you after*, but something held her back. Whether her conscience would allow her to agree to such a thing, despite the knowledge the children were desperate not to return, she did not know.

Her mind swung between what was legally right and what was morally just, the possibilities and probabilities sparring against one another in a huge conflict of emotion.

Sighing with frustration, Betty knew what she must do. Raising a hand to knock, she stepped forwards but her legs nudged against something in the darkness. She reached down, unsure what it could be, and found a box-shaped object. Something wrapped in paper and tied with a length of string lay atop it.

Surely not! thought Betty, but as she lifted the objects into the moonlight she saw they were as she feared: a battered cardboard suitcase and a brown paper parcel. The moonlight was too dim to allow her to read the details written upon the cardboard tags, but there was no need to do so. She knew instinctively to whom the baggage belonged.

At that moment, Betty did the only thing she could and turned to leave, the suitcase in one hand, the parcel tucked beneath her arm. A few steps from the doorway she looked back and saw the curtains twitch, a slither of light escaping as someone peeked out into the night before the blackout curtain was pulled across and darkness returned.

Betty shook with anger. *How could anyone do such a thing? They be children - poor, defenceless children in need o' love and attention*, she told herself. *What kind o' person does that?* But then she considered who was behind such an act and was not at all surprised. Suddenly the problems caused by rules and regulations, by space and sleeping arrangements, and by having two extra mouths to feed did not seem insurmountable any longer.

'Bloody woman,' she muttered, and with that, Betty Atkins strode down the gravel driveway and over the fields towards home.

The children waited on the track where it overlooked the beach. The night air was cooler now, their nightclothes covered by coats as they stood.

Betty approached them out of the darkness. 'You should be in bed,' she said reproachfully, but her tone suggested she was far from cross. 'Where's Phillip? Do he know you're out here?'

Maude shrugged. 'He said it were okay. Besides, Robert wanted to listen to sea.'

'Why do you have my things?' Robert's parcel was the last thing he expected to see, and he took it from Betty. He looked at the string around his belongings; it was tied loosely so the heel of a slipper poked through the brown paper, the parcel in danger of coming open, and he held it close. It was his only link to home and his mother, and the thought warmed him.

'They were waiting for me ont doorstep,' Betty said delicately. She handed Peggy the suitcase, not sure how the children would take such rejection, and was doubly cautious after Robert had run away earlier. 'No sign o' Mrs Barnforth though.' She put an arm around Robert's shoulders, aware she needed to be careful in what she said next. 'I think she be a mite cross after earlier, so it best you stay wi' us until she calms down. What say you?'

Robert nodded. 'She didn't want us anyway,' he said. His emotions loosened the stranglehold around his chest, allowing his heart to beat more freely, and at that moment the thought of not having to go back to Mrs Barnforth was all that mattered. 'Can we stay with you all the time?'

Betty was taken off-guard, unsure of how to proceed. She would need to speak to Mrs Forsyth, that was a given, but for now, it was not something the children needed to think about. *In case matters don't go as hoped*, she thought. *Poor kids. Why on earth they been put through all this?*

'I'll speak to someone about this int morning.' Betty spoke softly, hoping to ease their worries, and she hugged Robert in what she hoped was a gesture of reassurance. He put his arm around her, his grip tight.

'Come on, let's have you back in bed,' Betty said. 'Time be gettin' on. You got school tomorrow.'

* * *

The dunes dropped away to reveal the sea as a flat shadow against the darkness of the moonlit sky. Waves hissed over the shale far below, the sound carrying in the still night air as the tide washed to and fro. Midway to the horizon, a white light flashed briefly and then was gone, but Robert had seen it. He had been walking with one eye on the horizon line, transfixed by the beauty of the ocean. 'What was that?'

'What were what?'

Robert pointed. 'A light. There was a light out there.' The light flashed again, three times in quick succession. 'There! You see?' The group huddled together against the first chills of the evening and watched, but saw nothing more.

'Likely be a fishing boat,' said Betty. 'They moor up down coast at Whitby.' They stood for a minute, and when the night remained dark Betty shepherded the children along the path. 'Come on, who be for hot milk before bed?'

Robert walked slowly, his attention still focused upon the darkness until they rounded a bend and his view of the beach fell away. Had the light really been a fishing boat? What if it had been someone in need of help, someone adrift and desperate, or something even more important? He craned his neck, eager to see if the light returned, but found himself pulled along by the others, the prospect of hot milk and a warm bed suddenly very appealing.

The path fell to silence, leaving only the whisper of the ocean as waves rolled back and forth across the shale, moulding it the way an artist sculpts a block of stone or a slab of clay. Amidst the shadows, two men waited patiently, figures who sensed the path above them was now empty, and they made their way cautiously across the beach. Climbing through the dunes they paused to listen once more, then satisfied all was quiet, they snipped a hole in the barbed wire, crawled silently through, and vanished into the darkness like ghosts in the night.

Chapter 5

An excited group met them at the school gates the next morning, eager to hear first-hand how Robert had kicked Mrs Barnforth in the shins before she had 'put them out'.

Veronica and Vivienne hung back, their tall tale of *beastly and uncontrollable behaviour causing mother to fear for her safety, and for ours*, told in the shadows and secluded corners of the schoolyard. Those more supportive of the children reacted with disbelief towards their flowery recount, viewing the truth as likely to be far different from that being touted around.

Maude found the entire situation enthralling. She took great pleasure in stating her new friends *would be stayin' wi' 'er from now on*, although mother had agreed to nothing of the sort. That did not prevent Veronica and Vivienne from rushing home after school to report back on who had said what, their account of Robert's hero status amongst certain families something that caused Mrs Barnforth to seethe with anger.

Mark my words, those children will wish they had never crossed my path, Mrs Barnforth grumbled. *And as for that family, well, there will be opportunities, and I will deal with them in my own sweet way.* She nodded in agreement with herself, a twisted plan to show them up for what they were already forming in her mind. *Yes*, she thought, *just you wait*.

* * *

Maude led the way home to Bank Cottages along a route that avoided going anywhere near Ravenscroft House. It provided a commanding view of the coastline right down to Whitby in the south, the open fields stretching as far as the eye could see to the north.

Tractors and other farm equipment tended the fields, and as they passed, Maude pointed the land girls out by name, proud to show off that she knew them all. A tall lady with a big smile strode out across the field towards them. 'This be Mrs Greenside,' said Maude. 'She lets me call 'er Maggie when mother not around. I really like her.'

Maggie leaned upon the fence. 'Well, you must be evacuees from Bolshy's,' she said, smiling down at Peggy and Robert. It was more of a statement than a question, and the use of Mrs Barnforth's non-too polite nickname made them all giggle. It was rude and more than a little disrespectful, but Maggie wasn't known for being appropriate. Her outspokenness had landed her in trouble with Mrs Barnforth on more than a few occasions. 'By sounds o' it, you give Bolshy summat to chew on, and good on you, I say. Just wish I been there to see it.'

The children giggled, the cheekiness of the comment making Robert grin with embarrassment, and he hid the flush in his cheeks by bending to pull up his socks. His legs were too thin for the stretch in the wool to hold them up and they had fallen down as he walked. He'd have to tie them with a length of string if he wanted them to stay in place.

'Anyways, you best be gettin' home. Mrs Forsyth were calling round - that's why your ma's not 'ere. Went home a good hour ago, she did.' Maggie raised her eyebrows and leaned a little closer as though relinquishing a secret. 'Good job Bolshy don't know as she'd dock your ma's wages for time off, that be for sure.'

Maggie dipped a hand into the breast pocket of her dungarees and pulled out two hard-boiled sweets, her weekly ration which she always saved for Maude and Phillip on account of having no children of her own. 'Don't seem fair today,' she said, looking at all four children. 'I only have two.'

'Don't matter,' said Maude. 'We can all share anyway,' and she cupped her hands as Maggie threw the sweets over the fence. She caught them expertly.

They ran further along the coastal path, then took the cinder track that led them in through the gardens at the back of the cottages. Maude rushed through the kitchen door leaving Peggy and Robert on the doorstep. They felt hesitant, unsure what news they would find waiting for them, and somehow standing upon the threshold kept the possibility of returning to Mrs Barnforth remote.

Betty beckoned them inside. She had news, she said, and asked them to sit around the table, a glass of milk and a slice of bread and dripping waiting before each chair. Robert's stomach rumbled at the sight of it but he did not start eating. He was too nervous. He felt sick.

'Mrs Forsyth been this afternoon,' Betty said quietly. 'It seems Mrs Barnforth won't have you back, and no one else int village can take you.' She raised her eyebrows at Robert. 'It appears you've caused a stink an' a problem, young man; a stink that needed raisin' wi' that woman long time ago, and problem we can't leave unsolved.'

Robert slunk into his collar, but Betty did not want the boy to feel bad so she pressed on. 'So, we made a decision,' she said. 'There be conditions, mind you, but Peggy, if you follow Maude and learn ways o' feeding chicks and picking eggs, and Robert, you share Will's chores, both can stay here for foreseeable future.'

Robert's eyes flicked to his sister then back to Betty, a grin spreading quickly upon his face. 'Really?' he said, unable to believe what he had just heard. 'We can stay?' He needed to hear the words again. He daren't believe it was true.

'You can stay.' Betty's words were drowned out as the kitchen erupted into a frenzy of jumping and hugging, the air filled with squeals and screams of excitement. She was almost knocked from her chair as Robert flung his arms around her neck and squeezed. The hug told Betty how much her decision meant.

For the first time since leaving home, Robert felt as though he was welcome. Given a choice, he would rather be at home with his mother, but if he had to be with anyone else, it was with the friends he had made, and he sensed Betty was genuine. She was kind and gentle and couldn't be more of a contrast to Mrs Barnforth if she tried, and that suited Robert just fine. For the first time since arriving in Ravenscroft the thought of running home retreated, and the dead weight that had twisted the pit of his stomach relaxed its grip. He squeezed Betty once more in gratitude. 'Thank you,' he muttered, the tears free-flowing and heartfelt.

Betty held out an arm and the others joined in, squashing her until she thought she might burst. She disentangled herself and stood up, the happiness that filled the room true and full-bodied, something she had not felt since before the war, before the children's father had gone away to fight and everything had taken on such a dark and foreboding tone. Another wave of emotion burst upon them and Betty shushed everyone with a wave of a hand as she attempted to gain their attention. 'But that be not all to do round here on daily basis, mind you,' she said, 'so if you live under my roof, you contribute in all ways.'

Another wave of excitement rolled over the group and Betty grinned at the reaction before indicating the bread and dripping, and the cup of milk on the table before them. 'And you can begin by eatin' up what's put before you,' she said. 'While we might not 'ave as much as some folk, what we do 'ave can't be wasted. Miss Snootypants o'er yonder might not miss eighteen shillings and sixpence a week she's due for keepin' you, but pennies like that won't go amiss 'ere.'

Betty squeezed Peggy's hand where it had slipped into her own. 'Now shoo, and take bread and milk wi' you,' she said. 'Go on, get out o' kitchen. I 'ave things to do.'

Chapter 6

School turned out to be quite different to home. Here, children of different ages worked alongside one another rather than in single classes, but Robert and Peggy soon settled in and their teacher, Miss Fenwick, treated them both with kindly affection. Miss Danby, who had travelled with them from home, had been billeted in Whitby where she had been placed in one of the town's larger schools. They missed her, but she had promised to visit and see how they were doing.

They made friends quickly, with all but a few children accepting them as though they had always lived in the village. Only those whose mothers were part of Mrs Barnforth's 'inner circle' kept their distance, and that suited Robert and Peggy fine.

Veronica and Vivienne were all eyes and ears, and Robert made sure they heard what he wanted them to hear. He particularly enjoyed dropping misinformation he knew would stir Mrs Barnforth and cause confusion and unease, such as receiving a message to say their father had been awarded a medal for bravery and their mother was prepared to come and deal with Mrs Barnforth personally. He also revelled in showing Veronica and Vivienne another version of Churchill's V for Victory sign, his mischief earning him a ticking-off from Miss Fenwick and another from Peggy on the way home, but the opportunity had been worth it, and he took his scolding without argument.

While they had only been away from home for a few weeks, the peaceful days and lack of nighttime air raids created a sense of distance from the war. They still had the rules of blackout and rationing to follow, but food was more readily available and Betty's table was always more laden than Robert and Peggy's had been back home. The wide variety of fruit and vegetables, herbs, weeds and fungi growing wild and in Betty's lovingly tended garden meant food was plentiful, with her preserves acting as a popular form of black-market currency that would help stock her pantry through the long winter months ahead.

Village life was a quiet affair. The main road through the village square took little traffic other than the occasional tractor and official military vehicles, but street names and signposts had been painted over or removed as they had at home. Public information posters were displayed prominently in shop windows and on noticeboards, and windows had been taped with anti-blast strips to prevent flying glass in the event of an explosion. Sandbags were piled against the doorways of important buildings in readiness, yet despite a sense of calm and the uneasy belief that Hitler's advance would halt at the coast of France, there was a growing realisation that Great Britain was next.

* * *

Time passed steadily, another week taking the children closer towards the school holidays. The weather continued to be hot and dry, and walking home along the coastal path Robert watched the ocean with fascination. It rippled against the shoreline and he felt a longing to step down from the path and feel the water lap around his ankles. He only half-listened as Maude and Will chattered with Peggy, but his ears pricked up when they began discussing Carrion's Wood.

Maude told them Mrs Barnforth owned everything they could see, including the row of cottages where they lived, but not Carrion's Wood or the small plot of land before it. 'That's why Mrs Barnforth always be in such a bad mood. Mother say every time she steps out front door it remind 'er o' what she don't own.'

The wood sat above them now as they walked, a dark smudge against the horizon that watched their every step. 'Does anyone ever go up there?' asked Peggy.

Maude and Will shook their heads. 'We're not allowed,' she said. 'Who would want to anyway? Some nights I hear things. Mother says it just be tree spirits shiftin' furniture 'round, but I know she only tryin' to make me feel better.' She shuddered. 'I'll not go up there for owt.'

'Nor me,' said Will. 'Tommy Barnes bet me 'is gobstopper once to go but I turned 'im down. Didn't want it anyway. He been suckin' on it for week before he bet me.'

Peggy retched at the thought.

'But Robert's been,' said Maude, not thinking what she was saying.

'What was it like?' asked Will. 'You scared?'

Robert avoided the question. 'I won't go again.' He pointed to the beach instead. 'I want to go down there though. Never been on a beach.'

'Nobody's allowed,' said Maude. 'It's dangerous. Says so.' She pointed to the red and white sign spiked into the ground at the start of the beach path. Barbed wire was coiled beyond it like the skeleton of an unending snake.

'I won't go on the sand,' said Robert. 'I just want to see.'

'Robert, no.' Peggy faced her brother, Maude close by. Their faces showed how they felt about such an idea.

'You can't,' said Maude. 'If you do, we'll tell mother. She'll be right angry! She's forbid us go anywhere near beach.'

Will's words drove a dagger through their objections. 'I've been down,' he said. 'Three times.' Everyone looked shocked. How could he have been so reckless? 'Path be safe,' he said. 'It's just beach we can't go on.'

'No,' said Peggy again. 'Robert, you can't. I forbid it.'

Robert looked angrily at his sister. 'You're not my mother!' he snapped. 'You can't tell me what to do. Nobody can!'

Peggy's eyes filled with tears and her voice wavered. 'But I'm supposed to be looking out for you. I promised Mother I would, and I say you can't go.'

Robert sometimes found difficulty in deciding between what he should and could do. 'You can't stop me,' he said curtly, his strong will surfacing. It had led him into trouble on more than a few occasions.

Tell the lad he can't do something and he'll go out of his way to do the opposite. He's impulsive, his mother had once said when Robert had pushed a step too far.

His father had nodded in agreement. *He's strong-willed, that's for sure.*

And who does he take after for that?

Her eyes flared at Robert's disregard for common sense. 'Well, we're going to tell Betty!' she said indignantly, and with that, the girls turned and ran towards the cottages.

Once the girls were out of sight Will pointed to the path through the dunes. 'I'll show you if tha' wants,' he said. 'Come on.'

Chapter 7

Professor Frederick Barnforth took little interest in the running of Ravenscroft House. Such matters were best left in the capable hands of his wife as he busied himself either in his office or in London on 'Official Business'.

As a leading historian and expert in ancient languages, the Ministry of Defence had come to him at the outbreak of war. His expertise and research into 'matters best not discussed' kept him extremely busy, and as German forces tightened their stranglehold on Europe and prepared for their mass invasion of Britain, Professor Barnforth's research had become of even greater importance.

But his work had also drawn the attention of the German High Command, and in recent months the Professor had found himself in the company of visitors who suggested family members may be at risk if he was unwilling to provide the help they requested.

He had to tread carefully, that was a given - take a step in one direction and he betrayed his country, step the other way and he risked putting his family in danger with Nazi Germany. Either way, his family was at risk.

The conflicting sides of the decision had kept him awake night after night. Whichever way he looked at it, matters came down to a simple choice: Great Britain or Nazi Germany. Safety or risk. But then there was the archaeology.

He knew it was selfish to even consider the notion under the circumstances, but his entire life had been spent searching to uncover this one site of interest. It was more than work, it was a calling that went far beyond dedication and was the ultimate find, one that would piece together the tantalising threads of more than a thousand years of history. Until recently, the stories and clues he had uncovered had remained isolated from one another, the link between them absent, but now it seemed the past had offered him a crack into the window of history, a route into the past undiscovered by anyone else. How could he not consider such a possibility, even briefly?

Yet in the same breath, the present threatened to withhold it from him, whip it from his grasp and leave him with nothing. It seemed everything came down to a single painful question he did not know how to answer: was he prepared to allow his life's work to be used as a bargaining chip?

'It's time to pick your side, Frederick,' he told himself. 'It's time to make a choice.' But there were too many ifs and buts, too many possibilities that could push the outcome this way or that, and he sat with his head in his hands. Whichever choice he made would be painful, he just had to decide where his true loyalties lay.

*   *   *

Only when they were sure the Professor had left that morning did they move in. The house was empty, Mrs Barnforth and her girls having left before her husband, so apart from the housekeeper, they felt sure the house was quiet.

The men shuffled forward at a crouch, positioning themselves at the window. Due to the warm weather, the windows had been left slightly ajar, and that made the job of breaking in easier. All it took was the use of a narrow bar between window and frame to prise them apart, the splintering sound loud in the stillness but brief enough not to attract attention.

They knew exactly what they were looking for, and as one man listened at the door, the other went to the bookshelves and removed the leather-bound journal from its place. They left the way they had arrived, their actions unnoticed, the study undisturbed, the broken window the only evidence anyone had been there at all.

Chapter 8

Betty raced back along the path. Her heart thudded against her ribs, her stomach knotted and churning as she feared the worst. *Pigheaded boys!* she growled. *An' Will knows better, that be for sure. I'll tan lad's backside when I get 'im home. He won't sit down for next week!*

Maude and Peggy were yards behind, Betty's long legs outstripping them as she put on another burst of speed. Her feet went out from under her as she rounded the bend, the sandy path causing her feet to slide, and as she righted herself she saw two figures rushing towards her. She covered the final few feet and sank to her knees.

The boys stumbled as they spoke and gasped for air at the same time. Will steadied himself enough to finally become coherent. 'It's cut!' he stammered, pointing desperately back the way they had come. 'The wire, it's cut! It's been cut!'

Betty placed her hands on her son's shoulders, her eyes peering into his as she willed him to slow down and catch a breath. 'Cut? What do you mean, cut?' Her breathing was ragged but she pushed her anger aside as she looked between the boys. 'What's cut?' she repeated, somehow knowing what they were about to say. She coughed as dryness caught in her throat, though whether from her running, her anger or the implications of the boys' words, she could not say.

'The wire. The barbed wire!' shouted Robert. 'And there's blood!'

Maude appeared suddenly to one side of Betty, Peggy on the other. 'Blood?'

The boys nodded, their eyes wide, their faces panicked. Robert glanced back along the path as though expecting someone to lunge at him from the grass. He clasped his hands tightly, his body tense in readiness to defend himself. Will pointed again, his face filled with alarm. 'It's cut all way down.'

'Have you been down?' Betty's initial anger at the boys' behaviour changed to one of serious concern. She grabbed their hands and checked for cuts, for blood, but saw nothing. Both boys looked unharmed and she shook Will by his arms. 'The beach – 'ave you been down ont beach?' She knew it was supposed to be mined but didn't know for sure.

Will shook his head and looked to Robert for backup. 'We haven't,' said Robert. 'We went as far as the barbed wire, but it's cut. That's as far as we went. Honest!' His eyes were dark pools of fear.

'Show me!' Betty started forward and the boys took over. They ran to the sign and stopped just beyond it.

Will pointed down the embankment. 'Look!'

Betty moved cautiously, every step as light upon the sandy edge of the dune as she could manage. She held her breath as fear lodged itself at the back of her throat. The coils ran left and right, great loops of wire spiked into the ground with wooden stakes, their skin-tearing barbs terrifying to look at. And amongst the coils were gaps, deliberate openings where the wire had been cut and folded back on itself. Some of the barbs were discoloured like rust upon metal left out in the rain, but it was not rust. *Could be animal blood*, she thought.

Don't be ridiculous! she corrected herself. *Animals don't use wire cutters.*

*   *   *

Constable Goodwin had followed them back from the village, the Home Guard not far behind. They sat now in Betty's kitchen, steaming mugs of tea all round, the 'family discussion' about Will and Robert's choices like a bad smell that no one would admit to. That conversation would undoubtedly take place later, but for now, all they could do was wait. Any talk of the situation the boys had uncovered was firmly silenced by the constable, his response that it was

Official business an' best left alone until Home Guard 'ave assessed situation, putting the matter firmly to bed.

Captain Reed entered the kitchen a short time after. He was a slender gentleman with dark but thinning hair, his role as Captain of Ravenscroft's Home Guard taking priority over his daily role as the local butcher on any other day of the week. He stood with his cap tucked beneath his left arm, his swagger stick and leather gloves in his other hand. He cleared his throat,

'I would like to thank you all for your watchfulness today,' he began. 'Quite admirable, I must say. You are the eyes and ears this village needs. This country needs, in fact.' Despite being a local man, Captain Reed's voice lacked the strong North Yorkshire accent of his fellow villagers, his tone more rounded and authoritative. The boys knew the situation was serious. 'Might I ask what you were doing to make such a discovery?'

Robert shrunk in his seat, his usual bravado deserting him. Will's eyes went large. Neither boy had the confidence to speak up.

'Captain Reed asked a question,' Betty said. 'Show your manners and answer.' Her tone was firm. She wanted to hear their side of events as much as Captain Reed.

'We...' Will stumbled over his tongue. Robert swallowed hard.

'Boys?' Betty was adamant they be held to account over their actions, despite uncovering something of importance.

Maude took hold of her brother's hand beneath the table but he shrugged her off and she sat back, a smaller version of herself. She was only glad it wasn't her under the spotlight; she didn't think she could stomach any more upset, especially after Mother had welcomed them into the family and treated them so well. Robert had shown himself to be more settled in recent weeks because of it, and she could only hope the trouble he was in didn't undo everything he had achieved so far.

When he spoke it was quietly, his voice barely above a whisper. 'It was my fault. I wanted to go down to the beach.' His eyes searched for understanding in the faces around him. 'I've never seen the sea before.' His gaze came to rest upon Will and they looked at one another before Will took over.

'I told 'im I knew way down. Said I'd show 'im.' He looked over to his mother, his voice timid. 'I'm sorry.'

Betty nodded. Will wasn't a bad lad, never had been, he was just a bit impulsive at times.

Captain Reed took a small step closer to the table, all eyes upon him. 'You do understand the danger you put yourselves in today?' he asked. 'Barbed wire alone can be enough to inflict serious injury. That is why it's there. And as for the beach...' He angled his head, the intensity of his stare providing warning enough. 'You do know the beach is mined?' he asked.

Neither boy moved, the severity of their actions being drilled home. A reprimand by the Captain of the Home Guard carried extra weight over a telling-off by Betty.

'If you have gone down there in past, or even considered it, then heed my warning and don't. Stay on the path where it is safe,' the Captain said. 'The last thing we need is unnecessary injury, or worse.'

The boys nodded, their eyes full of fright, their hearts hammering as they considered the meaning behind his words. 'No, sir, we won't,' said Will quietly. Robert shook his head.

Captain Reed's stare lingered and discomfort rose in both boys, colour filling their cheeks until their faces burned. 'And mind you don't.' He held their gaze a moment longer, then turned to Betty. 'Right then. I'll be off,' he said. He glanced around at the faces once more. 'But thank you again, all of you, for your vigilance.'

Betty stood up and the children scraped their chairs back as they followed suit, their manners suddenly formal and important, their hands by their sides as though standing to attention. The last thing they wanted to do was add rudeness to the list of things to be discussed later.

'Mrs Atkins. Children. I bid you goodnight.' And with that, Captain Reed stepped towards the door.

'Thank you,' said Betty. 'You've certainly given children food for thought. Rest assured, there be no further off-track excursions. You have my word.'

Nothing further was said after Captain Reed left. The boys were directed straight to bed instead without supper, and they deemed it unwise to argue.

Betty had her say the next morning instead, the boys left in no doubt about her feelings. They listened in silent acceptance, promising to stay away from the beach and out of any kind of trouble, and considering themselves lucky to have escaped without further repercussions. There was much to do with it being the weekend, and for the next two days at least, Betty wanted the boys where she could cast her eyes over them.

The boys left to complete their chores after breakfast but were back for an early lunch, settling down afterwards to an afternoon indoors with the wireless for company. Saturday was usually a mixture of light music entertainment and news programmes for adults, with Children's Hour for the younger listener, but at 3.30pm Betty tuned the radio instead to a broadcast by the Prime Minister. The boys paid little attention, the girls even less so, much of Winston Churchill's powerful words and vivid language above their heads, but Phillip sat alongside his mother and she gripped his hand tightly throughout.

Churchill spoke in a clear and authoritative voice, every word tightening the grip around her heart, and she shushed the boys as they burst into laughter at some shared silliness. She took a deep breath to calm herself, releasing it slowly as the tension in Churchill's words increased to convey the gravest of messages.

The Battle of France is over. The Battle of Britain is about to begin.

And with that, war came to Ravenscroft.

Chapter 9

Betty sent the boys out the following morning once they had completed their chores. 'I want you out from under my feet,' she told them. 'I'm busy stewing and canning fruit, last thing I need is you gettin' int way.' She had remained tense since Churchill's speech the previous afternoon and had not slept well as a consequence, spending the night thinking and planning. If war was coming to their door she had a lot to do. 'But mind you keep to your promises,' she told them pointedly. 'And stay away from trouble.'

The boys went out with one eye permanently on the sky, the prospect of seeing planes in action never far from their minds. Robert remembered a German bomber flying low over Middlesbrough, smoke billowing from one of its engines as it struggled to remain aloft. The memory was exciting and he was eager for Will to see something similar for himself.

Will led them towards a place known locally as The Tops. Robert had heard it talked about at school and envisaged the remains of a castle, but wasn't sure quite what to expect.

'It be an old farm. Been there years, but there always be summat to dig up,' said Will. He walked backwards as he talked. 'All sorts o' places to climb an' all. Come on, it'll be fun. You'll love it.'

The Tops stretched inland from the coast to the north of Carrion's Wood. It meant they would have to pass by the trees and Robert wasn't too keen, but he remained quiet. He eyed the wood suspiciously as they neared it, but their route took them in a loop that ensured they kept their distance. He picked up a stick and whipped it back and forth through the long grass, imagining it to be a sword as he sliced the heads off long grasses and dandelions. Seeds fluttered on the breeze, their feather-like sails carrying them high as though escaping the world. Doing so lightened his mood and he whipped at them again with gleeful shouts.

Will lunged at Robert with a stick of his own. 'En-garde!' he called, their imaginary swords clashing against one another before Robert jabbed Will in the stomach and he fell to the ground in an exaggerated death, his arms laid out in the shape of a cross. A shadow, large and dark, cawed overhead as though laughing and Robert waved his make-believe sword at the bird, before standing poised over Will as though over a vanquished enemy. 'Just call me King Robert!' he grinned.

A sudden noise split the air, sharp and powerful like the splintering of wood, and a flock of ravens took to the air from the treetops. Their cries were stark and abrasive against the stillness of the morning and Robert froze. 'What's happening?' His legs trembled at the memory of being inside Carrion's Wood.

Will watched the birds with a frown. It was nothing unusual, but the sound was unexpected. 'Don't know,' he said, 'but it be the kind of thing that 'appens 'round 'ere.'

The crows settled within the trees, their noise reduced to a few raucous cries, but still the boys did not move on. Finally, Will took a few steps. 'Let's get past while all's quiet,' he said. 'Come on.'

They walked on for a while in silence, Will's chatter filled with boyish talk and daftness in an effort to distract his friend, but Robert's nerves were on edge and it showed. Will continued his effort. 'Can't stand Veronica and Vivienne,' he said with a wrinkle of his nose, the expression making him look like a pig. His eyes blazed at a remembered clash when they had blamed him for something he hadn't done. 'Cause trouble for everyone an' spoil fun, they do,' he said. He snorted in disgust. 'Don't think they knows how to have fun anyway. Would you, living at home wi' 'er for a mother?'

Robert grunted. The sound said everything.

Will put on a feminine voice. 'Oh, Veronica! Oh, Vivienne, my little sweet pea, come to mummy!' he mimicked.

'I bet their idea o' fun be sittin' round fireplace castin' spells.' Robert sniggered, yet beneath everything a tremor fluttered across his heart. He eyed Carrion's Wood one more time, then forced himself to turn his back upon it.

The faint sound of an engine drifted on the breeze and the boys looked around, expecting a tractor or some other vehicle, but the glint of light on metal flashed high above them. The drone of another engine joined it, the pitch of both engines discordant like musical notes not intended to be played together, yet as one, the glinting dots danced spirals overhead.

A sharp staccato rattled over the drone of the engines, its repetitive tat-tat-tat-tat-tat sounding again and again until one of the dots flared and began a slow fall towards the earth. A ribbon of smoke trailed behind it, thin at first before thickening into a tongue of flame that curved across the sky like the fury of a burning serpent.

The boys watched in awe as the aircraft fell. British or German, they had no idea, but its fall took it below the horizon. Others twisted and turned, a deadly ballet of grace and skill that left intricate chalk patterns across the sky.

'Whoa!' cried Robert. 'You see that?'

'Yeah.' Will drawled, his head spinning with the spectacle overhead. Planes darted and dived, angry fire raging between them before another began its fall from the heavens.

A low growl made them look to the horizon. Nothing revealed itself at first, the bright sunlight having whitened their vision after staring upwards for so long, but as their eyes adjusted they became aware of a small shape skimming the ground towards them. Its wings drew a straight line, its yellow engine cowling bright in the sunshine. Smoke billowed and churned behind it, the engine stuttering as it misfired and began to falter. A second aircraft shadowed it higher and to the left, its profile less square with a more subtly rounded form. The roar of their engines increased by the second.

'They ours?' asked Will.

Robert stared into the brightness. 'Not sure, but he looks like he's going to crash.' He grabbed Will and dragged him back into the undergrowth, but Will resisted. 'Get down!' Robert yelled. He pulled at his friend again and they tumbled to the side of the track as a German aircraft, its fuselage clad in grey and green camouflage, bore down upon them.

The pilot did his best to keep the aircraft airborne, but the ME 109's ailing bulk fought back and the pilot struggled to steer it away from the boys. Their two countries may be at war, but the pilot believed children were off-limits when it came to the enemy. He banked the plane to the left, the black crosses emblazoned across its wings and fuselage visible as it skimmed a hedge and ploughed into the grassland beyond. Its propeller scattered plumes of grass, earth and dust into the sky as the blades dug into the ground, the force of impact twisting them backwards and stalling the engine. The plane slid on, scouring a trench of destruction in its wake.

The Spitfire that had shadowed the Messerschmitt down roared overhead. With his enemy on the ground he circled, the sound of his engine more of a purr than the rough growl of the ME 109, and the pilot looked down on the boys. He gave them a jaunty wave and grinned, then clipped his oxygen mask back into place, gunned his engine and raced skywards once more. His work was far from over.

All noise ceased and the boys raced to the hedge. The Messerschmitt sat amidst a cloud of dust and debris, a battered relic that showed no sign of movement. They assumed the pilot had been killed in the crash, but the canopy soon swung open and a figure clambered out. Moments ago the pilot had been in the sky, now he was on firm ground. Enemy ground.

Robert and Will scrambled through a gap in the hedge and raced forwards, but stopped suddenly when they saw a figure standing behind the pilot.

It was Carrion.

He was an imposing figure in a simple knee-length linen shift, washed-out and discoloured with age, patched and threadbare in places where it had worn through. A long-sleeved vest, which may once have been dark, fell to his wrists, its wide cuffs raggy and tattered. A knotted twist of leather around his waist pulled the shift up from his boots while a cloak hung clasped at his shoulders, its colour dark like the feathers of his beloved ravens.

The old man's face was thin and lined with age, his skin tanned and rugged-looking from years spent living outdoors, but his eyes were piercing and intelligent. He observed everything from under brows that matched his greying hair, wild and unkempt, yet there was a sense of trustworthiness about him, of service and valour. The children sensed he was not the figure he had been made out to be.

Carrion leaned upon his staff as he eyed the pilot. Ravens flapped and cawed around him, their noise deafening, the pilot's sudden appearance having unsettled them, but Carrion's presence was reassuring and they soon calmed.

The pilot turned, aware for the first time of the old man, and unclipped his parachute harness without taking his eyes from him. Robert and Will ran closer, Betty's words of caution and concern for their safety ringing in their ears but they ran on regardless. This was an enemy soldier, after all, someone whose intent was to cause damage to their country, their family and their friends. They knew being so close was dangerous, but they were here and it was exciting.

The pilot looked warily between the boys and the old man. He had no intention of becoming a prisoner of war, his mind focused on evading capture for as long as possible, and he took a step backwards. He was in no doubt he could outpace anyone who decided to follow.

When Carrion spoke his voice was commanding, his instruction clear upon the still air. 'Remain,' was all he said. Ravens took to the air noisily as he spoke, sensing his change of mood, their behaviour anxious and unsettled once again.

The pilot's mistake was to back away another step, and as he did so, Carrion lifted his staff and stepped quickly forward. He repeated his command, and when the pilot did not do as instructed, Carrion swept the legs from under him with his staff. The movement was blindingly fast and ravens flocked around the fallen man, their beaks pecking painfully at his head and shoulders as though chastising him for his lack of obedience. They retreated slowly, leaving the pilot bloodied upon the ground and Carrion stepped forwards. He levelled his staff at the man's face. 'Remain,' he repeated.

The pilot made to stand and Carrion struck him again, this time across the back. He fell forwards and cried out in pain, the ravens falling upon him in attack once more before quickly withdrawing. When he next sat up, bloodied and scratched, he was holding a pistol. He pointed it directly at Carrion.

Robert and Will scrambled backwards, the sight of the gun terrifying. That was when the pilot spoke.

'Bleibzurück!' he said firmly. *Stay back!*

Carrion struck the pilot again, hard and fast across the head this time, and the German stumbled. Blood oozed from a cut to his cheek where the blow had landed. The pilot was not happy. 'Bleibzurück!' he shouted, and when Carrion raised his staff a third time the pilot fired.

The birds went wild, attacking the pilot with their beaks and talons, but the bullet passed straight through the old man and kicked up a plume of dirt where it embedded itself in the earth behind him. Carrion flinched slightly but did not fall. There was no sign of blood and he raised his staff as the pilot fired a second time.

'No!' shouted Robert, horrified at the scene he was witnessing. His eyes filled with tears, but what could he do? Will stood by him, his mouth open in shock. The boys suddenly felt weak and vulnerable. Why hadn't they listened to Betty's advice?

Again Carrion flinched, but the bullet left no mark and drew no blood. It was as if the bullet had missed, but the boys had seen them strike the old man, leaving holes in his shift where they had struck.

The pilot hesitated, expecting the old man to stagger and fall, but when he remained standing the pilot was taken aback. His fingers curled more tightly around the handle of the pistol and he stood, unsure how to proceed. Within that moment, Carrion raised his staff and struck a sharp blow to the pilot's head. He slumped to the ground and knew no more.

*　*　*

Betty watched in horror as a German fighter came in low over the village. A Spitfire dropped in behind it, cannons blazing, and the Messerschmitt belched a cloud of black smoke. The air hung heavy with its oiliness as the aeroplane lost power and dropped towards the surrounding fields, its descent the final act of its war.

She knew the boys were somewhere in the direction the plane was about to come down, but surely they wouldn't be anywhere nearby? Unease filled her chest as she set off in search of them, Maude and Peggy running to keep pace with her. Between them, there was a good chance they would find them.

They won't go anywhere near, she told herself. *They knows better than that.*

The boys were shocked. They had just seen a man shot twice, but the bullets had passed straight through him.

Carrion stood a little distance apart. He kept guard as though nothing had happened, and although the boys knew it was impossible, the right thing to do now was to check on him. He had protected them. It was their turn to look after him now.

They walked slowly forwards, but despite what Betty had told them about keeping their distance, they felt safe. Ravens wheeled overhead, agitated and noisy, but the old man calmed them with a soothing noise. The birds settled, one landing on his shoulder and watched the boys through beady, unblinking eyes.

The old man leaned on his staff at the boys' approach. He did not speak and Robert and Will looked at one another as they pondered their next move. They had both been taught to speak politely to their elders, but nothing had prepared them for this.

'Sir, are you hurt?' Robert's voice trembled, although he tried his hardest to maintain a level tone.

Carrion stared intently as though weighing them up and the boys exchanged glances. Robert cleared his throat, his voice a little stronger the second time. 'Sir, are you hurt?' he repeated.

Carrion shook his head. When he spoke, his voice was strong but tinged with age. 'I have fought many battles. Such a minor skirmish holds little fear.'

'But he shot you,' chipped in Will, a touch more sharply than he had intended. He still could not believe the old man was unhurt.

Carrion's eyes took in both boys. He straightened and patted his body. 'I appear to be uninjured,' he said, then glanced behind him and settled his old frame down upon a weathered tree stump, the action accompanied by a sound of effort. He planted his staff between his feet and fixed the boys with an intense stare.

The ravens burst into a flurry of activity as Will moved forward, their wings taking them skyward. Only when he retraced his steps did they settle once again. 'But what about pilot?' he said across the distance. 'Shouldn't he be arrested or summat?'

Carrion glanced at the motionless figure of the pilot and nodded. 'Worry yourselves not, young sirs. Fetch your masters and soldiers, I will watch over him until then.' He flicked his head in the direction of the village. 'Now go.'

Robert and Will raced back towards the village. The most direct route took them west across the fields towards the main road, then downhill past Ravenscroft House. Robert was reluctant to go anywhere near the house at first, but Will explained it was the quickest way into the village. Their need to raise the alarm was more important than anything else, and even if they saw Mrs Barnforth there would be no reason to stop.

The village lay before them. It was an idyllic scene of country life, but looking upon it they realised nobody would guess the events they had just witnessed, nor would anyone dare to imagine the truths that were about to unfold in the coming days.

Two figures appeared on the track before them. They were silhouetted by the sun and the boys found it difficult to see any detail as they passed, but one of them pulled the cuff of his jacket down as though to conceal his hand. His Good morning was clipped and formal, as though forced. Even Robert, who was only beginning to understand how local people talked, found it strange, but they returned the men's greeting. It would have been rude not to.

'Who are they?' asked Robert.

Will shrugged. 'Dunno. Never seen 'em before, but they sure don't look right.'

Chapter 10

The arrest of a German pilot caused much interest and in some cases anger from the locals. Villagers watched as he was brought into town under guard, and after being treated for his injuries by the local doctor, a temporary cell was made for him in the Town Hall. An armed unit of regular soldiers arrived soon after to take him away, and Ravenscroft returned to its peaceful way of life.

Betty Atkins was not happy. 'Trust you both to be in middle o' things.'

Peggy listened, unable to believe her brother was in trouble again. What would their mother think? She fixed him with her best older sister stare but he didn't seem to notice.

'And Carrion?' she added. She shook her head in dismay. 'Do you not listen to anythin' I tells you?' She stood up and walked to the kitchen sink, refolded a tea towel that was already folded, then returned to her seat. 'Let me get straight end o' this, because I be strugglin' to understand what you're tellin' me,' she said. She flapped a hand in the air as she attempted to find a way into the conversation, and when she couldn't find a thread that made sense she went back to the explanation the boys had given her. 'You say pilot shot Carrion and bullets went right through 'im like he weren't there?'

The boys nodded. It was the truth. What else was there to say?

'And you expect me to believe such a story?' Betty had begun her conversation by reminding the boys that the truth was the best option in any situation, but despite the ridiculous way the story sounded, they nodded.

'And yet he were unhurt?'

They nodded again. It was the truth after all, not that anyone appeared to believe them.

'Pfff!' Betty exhaled in exasperation.

'But it's true!' blurted Robert. He couldn't help his outburst.

Oh, no! thought Peggy. *Here we go again. Didn't you learn your lesson the first time?*

'We couldn't just leave him,' Robert added. 'We had to check he wasn't hurt.'

'It's were same thing you would've done,' said Will, framing Betty with the comment and knowing he was right. It was a dangerous game to play, but worth the risk of Betty exploding at the cheek of her son's insolence.

Betty was caught between a rock and a hard place. It was exactly the kind of behaviour she had instilled in her children since they were old enough to know right from wrong, but that didn't make what they had done any easier. 'Can't you see I'm tryin' to keep you safe?' she said, 'and don't even me get started on why you were there int first place. If plane had hit you or exploded – '

'We didn't know it were going to crash,' said Will. 'How could we?' Robert shook his head in agreement.

Betty looked at the boys and sighed. They had a point, checking on Carrion was precisely what she would have done, regardless of the risk, and she had always prided herself on having brought up her family to uphold the values she held so dear. The story still smacked of boyhood misbehaviour, but she would just have to take it at face value for the moment. No doubt the truth would reveal itself at some point.

'Okay,' she said at last, 'but we're all going into village together this afternoon. We need groceries and you're to stick by my side. It don't seem as though either o' you can be trusted out o' sight for five minutes these days.' She looked them in the eye. 'Let's try an' have afternoon where nothing upsets apple cart, shall we?'

Robert and Will stood outside Griffiths' while Betty queued to stock up on the weekly rations. She chatted with other ladies as they waited, the main topic of conversation about the captured German pilot, but Robert also heard his name mentioned at one point. Betty indicated him with a tilt of the head and all eyes turned towards him, causing him to shrink away, his face red with embarrassment at being talked about.

The conversation continued and Robert turned his back in what he hoped wasn't considered a rude gesture. He sunk his neck inside his collar and tried to make himself look invisible before sliding a few steps further along the wall.

The street before them was all but empty. Only a few afternoon shoppers moved between doorways, the village having a limited number of shops. Betty had sent Peggy and Maude on an errand, but the boys had been given no such luxury - not that they would have wanted an errand anyway - and they stood around kicking their heels in boredom.

Robert picked at the iron stubs which were all that remained of the iron railings. The government had ordered them removed and melted down to build tanks, bombs and bullets, and as he fingered their sawn edges he recoiled suddenly, blood dripping from his finger. He sucked at the wound while Will laughed. 'Daft beggar,' he said, and grinned as Robert inspected the cut. The bleeding gave no sign of lessening and he pressed on it with his thumb to stem the flow.

Betty left the shop with most of what she needed. She was late shopping today and so was short of a few items. At least she had fresh-grown produce to fall back on and would be able to trade to make their rations go further. 'Come on,' she said. The boys trawled behind, their interest anywhere but the drudgery of shopping.

Vehicles were few and far between in Ravenscroft under normal circumstances, and during wartime the majority were military, so when a car crawled past, Robert looked up. Mrs Barnforth peered angrily through the windscreen as though looking for someone to blame for her mood, and when she locked eyes with him, she braked with no concern for any other road users. She slammed the door behind her and pointed at Robert. 'You! Don't move!'

Robert felt the blood drain from his face. He looked at Betty in panic and saw her step to the left so the boys were shielded behind her. Quite what Mrs Barnforth's issue was this time they did not know, but Betty was instantly set for the inevitable battle which was about to unfold. She opened the conversation in an overly polite tone, hoping to calm the situation before it erupted out of hand. She doubted it would prove effective, but had to be worth a try. 'Good mornin', Mrs Barnforth. Is there problem we can 'elp you with?'

Mrs Barnforth was not about to be swayed that easily. 'Don't you good morning me!' she shouted. She stood to the side of Betty, her eyes fixed upon Robert where he stood shielded behind her. His face was ashen, his expression a mask of worry. He had seen Mrs Barnforth's aggressive manner before and did not wish to experience it again. 'You – get to the front where I can see you, you little thief!'

Betty took to Robert's defence instantly. 'Ah – ah,' she said. 'What did you just call the boy?'

'I speak as I find, Mrs Atkins, as you very well know, and a thief is what that boy is. A thief. Now, move aside!' She reached out for Robert's arm, dismissing Betty as a teacher might dismiss an unruly pupil. 'Put yourself where I can see you!' she said angrily.

'Oh, no tha' don't!' Betty deflected Mrs Barnforth's hand and pushed Robert further behind her. 'Don't you go treatin' lad like that!' It was Betty's turn to dismiss Mrs Barnforth. 'I care little for who you are and what you think he's done, but he be my responsibility now. Your opportunity to treat lad wi' dignity vanished when you threw 'im out!'

A crowd had begun to gather and an audible gasp went up at Betty's claim. Bystanders turned to one another, shocked to hear such an allegation said aloud, but glad to have it confirmed. The village rumour mill had been turning quicker than usual in recent days, and the public airing of dirty laundry before them was quite the spectacle. The crowd huddled shoulder-to-shoulder, their whispered comments and nudges drawing them closer as they awaited the next exchange.

Mrs Barnforth turned the accusation to her own benefit. 'Well, if you had bothered to reign the child in and teach the moral behaviours expected, we would not be standing here now!' she said with a smugness she believed was justified.

The crowd mumbled then fell silent again, but Betty was not prepared to stand for such an allegation. 'And if you did not stick your nose int air quite so much, p'rhaps you would see lad be in need o' love and attention,' she said. '*Love thy neighbour as thyself*, it says int bible, do it not, Mrs Barnforth? Well, you should heed those very words wi' a bit more care. You be quick enough to stand up in church on Sunday and read word of God, p'rhaps you should take such words to 'eart and stand by 'em a little more honestly int future.'

Robert and Will listened to the exchange in wide-eyed fear and curiosity, frightened to witness such an argument and unsure where it would finish up. And then Mrs Barnforth stooped to a new low, even for her. 'You're a fine one to talk of morals,' she said. 'turning up in the village, an unmarried mother looking for work and lodgings. If it wasn't for me – '

The crowd erupted into gasps of horror at Mrs Barnforth's disclosure, her intention to cause pain and embarrassment for Betty obvious, and it had worked.

Betty's face reddened at the public exposure of such personal details. The accusation was uncalled for and those who stood by bristled, their disgust at Mrs Barnforth's behaviour turning those who might once have overlooked her behaviour against her now. It was known only between a few that Betty had come to the village as a young unmarried mother, but she had met and married a local man and was as much a part of the village now as anyone else. She was well-liked, and for something so scandalous to be publically aired was simply malicious. Mrs Barnforth had just driven a wedge between herself and many of the locals which she would find difficult to repair.

Looking down, Betty saw the confusion in her son's eyes. He did not understand the implications of what had been said - or so she thought - and Betty was pleased. The time to tell him would come, but this was not the way. She opened her mouth to speak, to lead Mrs Barnforth's conversation elsewhere, but Mrs Barnforth was quicker off the mark. She left her previous comments to sting while she went back to her initial question. 'So, I will ask, and I want an answer: Why were you at my house?'

Her house? Robert didn't answer; how could he? He hadn't been there since the fateful evening when all the trouble had started a few weeks before. Panic filled his chest and tears brimmed. 'I... I haven't. We weren't,' was all he managed to say, his voice tight, his words strangled by fear. His pained expression said everything.

'There, and that be good enough for you! If Robert say he weren't there, then lad's word be good enough for me.' Betty was visibly upset by Mrs Barnforth's hurtful reveal but remained prepared to defend her family, and that now included Robert. 'Now, leave us be.' She stepped back and put an arm around each of the boys.

'You were seen,' retorted Mrs Barnforth. 'You were seen running away, the both of you. I saw you with my own eyes.' She turned to those watching, a finger pointing accusingly at Robert and Will. 'These boys broke into my husband's study this afternoon.' She drew herself up and stuck out her chin with indignation. Her voice remained angry, although it had lost some of its initial volume. She had won the first battle with Betty Atkins and was pleased with herself.

Those who stood by did not agree, and had heard enough. 'But why would lad take somethin' from your 'usband?' asked one. 'He's 'istorian or some such learned thing. What interest would that hold for lad?'

'The reason why is of little interest,' responded Mrs Barnforth. 'That they were seen running away is proof enough. They are thieves; thieves and troublemakers both,' she added.

Betty almost choked. The accusation had gone from thieves to thieves and troublemakers. She was mortified to have that said about her family; everyone who knew them knew that was not true.

'And when were this?' asked a voice from the crowd. Mrs Appleby had never been fond of Mrs Barnforth, and this opportunity gave her good reason to speak out. 'And what, accordin' to you, were boys doin' other than running?' She looked around at the ladies and gentlemen that stood with her. 'Boys don't walk anywhere,' said Mrs Appleby. 'Mine certainly don't. They run, it's what they does.' People nodded their agreement, a chorus of *mine too* and *typical boys* filled the pause. 'You catch boys inside your 'usband's study? You actually see 'em there?'

Mrs Barnforth did not appreciate being questioned and her face said as much. She glared at those who had dared to challenge her, and for the first time felt the tide begin to turn.

The war of words between the adults was too vicious for the boys to become involved in. While they were wary of speaking out further, others had begun supporting their innocence, and that gave Will confidence.

'We weren't there,' he said. 'We were on Tops when plane came down. We ran across fields then down High Road past Ravenscroft House to barn at Beck's Corner. Captain Reed were coming uphill wi' men and we told 'em where to find crash. Ask 'im, he'll tell you same thing.'

Will looked directly at Mrs Barnforth, eager to make his point but not wanting to inflame the argument further. 'We didn't leave road and we didn't go anywhere near Ravenscroft House,' he said. 'And that be truth.'

Despite the overwhelming support shown by the local townsfolk, Robert and Will were worried they would continue to be blamed for the break-in. They sat with Betty beneath the large Oak tree which dominated the village green and waited for Maude and Peggy to return. The shade was welcome, and not simply because of the warmth of the day – the tree's lofty branches provided strength and protection, as though offering a sense of wisdom as it listened to their conversation.

The earlier embarrassment still plagued Betty, but she did her best to settle the boys' fears and pushed her own emotions aside. 'Folks believe you,' she said, 'and so do I. You've no cause to worry.' She smiled. 'Folk rallied, and they don't do that for just anybody. You may be new, Robert, but you've fit in well an' folk like you.' She glanced towards the marketplace. 'Barnforth won't get far wi' lies like that, an' rightly so.'

Betty's eyes were steely, her face determined. 'The more you stand up to bullies, less power they 'ave. My old dad used to say that, and it be mighty good advice, believe you-me.' Her eyes were distant for a moment as she remembered her childhood. 'You'd do well to remember that.'

She patted the boys on the leg and turned as Peggy and Maude approached. They giggled between themselves, oblivious to everything and everyone, and Betty was glad to see it. The girls had struck up a solid friendship and it was as good for Maude as it was for Peggy. Their closeness provided the support each girl needed in such troubled times.

Betty took the paper bag Maude carried. She did her best to make do and mend whenever possible, trading eggs from her chickens and vegetables from the garden for other bits and pieces, as everyone else had taken to doing, but some things had to be bought. It was just the way things were, a necessity. And now with two extra children to clothe, matters had proved to be that much more of a challenge.

'Right then,' Betty said, drawing a line beneath events. 'I think it best you four disappear for a while. Go play but stay out o' trouble.' No doubt the girls would hear the story from the boys, but for now, Betty sent them off in the direction of the stepping stones. The river there was shallow, shin-high at most, and the local children often gathered there to splash around. It was also out of the village so there was little chance of bumping into Mrs Barnforth along the way. Betty was concerned over how the boys would react should they be confronted by her again.

Robert and Will's concern for Betty did not go unnoticed. 'What were that about?' whispered Maude once they had left their mother's hearing. She had sensed the atmosphere between them, despite their mother's best efforts to hide it, and she wanted to know. She could be like a dog with a bone when she wanted to be.

'Nothin' for you,' said Will. His answer was abrupt and final. He gave a sidelong glance at Robert, but Maude wasn't so easily fooled. She glanced at Peggy who in turn nudged her brother. His expression was clear: *Not talking.* Robert could be so stubborn at times. Peggy found that side of her brother infuriating.

'I'm not daft,' said Maude, 'so don't treat me likes I am.' She fell into step alongside her brother. 'Mother be upset over somethin'. What you been up to now?'

'I said it were nothin'! Anyway, why's it always my fault?' snapped Will. 'You do plenty wrong, but Mother don't seem to find out, or don't want to know!' He shook his head. 'Just keep your neb out!'

Will stomped off, leaving Maude to fume behind him. The girls moved together, their shared annoyance bubbling between them. 'They've been up to something, I can tell by the way Robert's avoiding me,' said Peggy. 'He always does that when he's in the wrong. Drives mother mad too.' For a moment she looked sad. 'Dad can always get him to talk though.'

'Yeah,' said Maude, 'I know what you mean.' She snorted in disgust. 'Brothers!'

Chapter 11

The stepping stones were on the far side of St. Thomas', the old Chapel that had served Ravenscroft since medieval times. The river over which the stepping-stones crossed passed through several villages on its way to the sea, Ravenscroft being the last, before it tumbled over a series of small falls and joined the River Esk outside Whitby.

It shallowed as it ran past the churchyard, allowing the stepping stones to connect the village with the farms on the opposite bank. It was a popular place amongst the local children and the ideal location for stick-boat races and dam-building.

Will and Maude knew the proper route to the stones was to walk around the churchyard. Cutting through was quicker, but Reverend Salter often sent them back out to walk all the way around, *This is a holy place, not a playground* ringing in their ears. That did not seem to stop them sneaking through whenever the opportunity arose, however, and today was no exception.

Will crept in through the gate and paused between the first of the yew trees that lined the path towards the main door. In days gone by, local men going off to fight in the crusades had made their bows from the trees. They had also sharpened their swords inside the church, leaving vertical gouges in the sandstone before having their weapons blessed at the altar. On their return they had added a cross mark to the first, recording the completion of their holy quest. The fact that so many marks remained incomplete was a stark reminder of the sadness and futility of war.

The sword marks had always fascinated Will. On many an occasion he had enjoyed running his fingers over them, imagining he could feel their history, but today his attention was elsewhere. He crouched behind a headstone as he heard voices. Robert ran forward at a crouch and squeezed in alongside him, the girls behind headstones to their left. 'What is it?' said Robert? 'Who – '

Will put a finger to his lips and urged everyone to listen. He pointed towards the side of the Chapel. 'Somebody's there,' he mouthed. 'If they see us we'll be in trouble for cuttin' through graveyard.'

'I don't hear – ' whispered Maude, but stopped mid-sentence as a voice reached her. It was low, not quite a whisper, but quiet enough to be easily missed.

Robert pointed again to the corner of the building. Will nodded and moved from his half-seated position to a squat, then dashed to the headstone in front.

'Robert, no!' hissed Peggy. She raised herself to her knees as though to follow, then thought better of it and dropped low again. Robert slid in behind a headstone and turned his back to it. He grinned, his recklessness infectious, and one by one the others crept the length of the chapel to regroup alongside him. The headstones gave perfect cover, the voices louder now and distinct against the birdsong, but despite being so close the voices remained unclear.

A large tomb stood back from the path, a monument to someone who had once lived well but who was now largely forgotten. Time had caused the structure to sink at one corner, its bulk settling year by year into the soft ground. From behind it, the children would have a clear view of the rear of the building whilst having cover amongst the summer grass that had sprouted up around it. In recent months the graveyard's upkeep had been neglected due to more important wartime issues, and that made it the perfect place from which to observe.

Will led the way. Robert followed, the girls more hesitant, but after seeing the boys hide amongst the long grass they crossed the short distance and squeezed in beside them. Just beyond the corner stood two men. Both were tall, one dark-haired with a neatly trimmed moustache and round spectacles, the other blonde and clean-shaven. Will recognised the men instantly from earlier in the day. 'It's them!' he mouthed.

'Who?' The shadow of the church shielded the men, the overhanging trees creating a screen and Robert struggled to see.

'We passed 'em on 'illside!' hissed Will. 'It's men we said didn't fit round 'ere.'

Robert shifted his position but found his view still obstructed, then one of the men stepped out from behind the tree cover and he saw a blonde-haired man. His left hand was bandaged. Will was right!

Maude nudged her brother and tipped her head towards the men. 'Who are they?'

'They spoke to us after German were shot down,' said Will. Peggy and Maude drew close to him as he whispered, their faces almost touching. 'Somethin' funny about 'em, though. They just out o' place.'

Peggy knew it was wrong to eavesdrop, but she squinted against the glare of the sun nevertheless. 'Could just be visitors,' she suggested.

'Nah, folk like that stand out,' said Will. He furrowed his brow and made a circle in the air with his finger. 'There nobody round 'ere we don't know.' He studied the men again. 'I tell you, they not locals.'

The more Peggy watched them, the more she had to agree. Their clothes and the way they stood, even the way they moved seemed wrong.

One of the men laughed, the joke between them enough to create movement, and the children quickly laid low to listen. To discover anything they would need to be cautious. And clever.

The men talked again in hushed voices, their words unintelligible before another voice joined them. It was deeper with a well-spoken English tone. 'Dr Piper says, 'Good morning."

The reply was equally formal but forced, rehearsed as though trying to behave in a certain way. 'Dr Wilmott sends his greetings.'

The children looked at one another.

Who?

The conversation continued, their words a little clearer. 'Thank you for your assistance, Herr Barnforth. The Führer will not forget this.'

The use of a single word was enough to throw the children into a state of panic. Will's face registered shock, his eyes wide. He couldn't believe what he had just heard and he leaned in close to whisper. 'Führer ?' he said. 'You hear that?'

Robert nodded. 'Yeah.'

Maude risked a glance and saw the third man side on. He faced inwards as they talked but remained partly secluded by low-hanging branches. She tapped her brother and pointed. 'Is that Professor Barnforth?'

Will stole a glance he hoped would go unnoticed. 'Looks like him,' he said, 'but what's he doing here?' His eyes sparkled at knowing something secretive, something important. 'You think he's Nazi?'

Robert shrugged his shoulders. 'Dunno. Maybe.' He watched a little longer and saw the man with the bandaged hand take a book from his pocket. He passed it to Professor Barnforth who leafed through it, stopping at a particular page as though familiar with its contents to point something out. The men chatted, the words *relics* and *fragments* used several times to explain something in the pages of the book.

Robert felt his heart miss a beat. What if the book had been taken from Professor Barnforth's study and they had attempted to deflect the blame onto someone else? What if the professor had been in on the scheme all along? After all, he knew precisely where to look in the book, as though it had been his to begin with. But why would thieves give it back to the professor after going to all the trouble of stealing it? None of it made sense.

He shuffled back through the long grass, eager to find a better place from which to listen. He inched away to Will's right and knelt with his shoulder to a headstone that stood a little closer, peering around its edge while the men continued to talk. After a short time, the man with the bandaged hand replaced the book in his coat pocket and patted it.

The group appeared to be breaking up, their secretive meeting concluded, but just as Professor Barnforth turned to leave he registered movement in the corner of his eye. He glanced around, his gaze taking in the wilderness of the overgrown graveyard, and that was when he saw Robert.

The professor did not recognise the boy, but he did recognise two of the other faces that stared out at him from the long grass: the Atkins' children, although the third face with them, a girl, he did not know. No matter, the professor knew he and his contacts had been seen, and that was a problem. What if their discussions had been overheard? What if that information was passed on? They had to be stopped.

He directed the bespectacled man to intercept the children from the right while the man with the bandaged hand ran directly towards them. The Professor set off in an anti-clockwise direction, intending to pin the children in on three sides and cut off any hope of escape.

Robert jumped up and back-peddled, initially unsure which way to go. Peggy and Maude screamed, their voices panicked and frightened as the men raced towards them, and Will shouted for them to run away to his left. Robert grabbed at Will's arm and together they stepped over vases of flowers and stone urns, hoping they would not trip as the men weaved their way through the gravestones.

The boys were quick and Professor Barnforth had not counted on the speed and agility of childhood. 'Come here!' he commanded, but the boys had taken off in one direction, the girls in another, with no intention of stopping.

The blonde-haired man lashed out and the boys ducked as his arm snatched the air above their heads. He snarled as he rounded the headstone, and in a sudden burst of speed was almost upon them. The man's agility took the boys by surprise, and as he ran at them again they split up.

Will squeezed through a narrow gap between two leaning headstones while Robert sprinted towards a pair of stone crosses that bordered a thickly wooded area against the churchyard wall. There was open space around the crosses and he stood before them as he turned to face his attacker.

Peggy ran into open space but slowed as her brother stood his ground. 'What are you doing?' she shouted. 'Run!' Her heart hammered with fear and her breath caught in her throat.

Will turned to see the blonde-haired man bearing down on his friend, and for a moment considered running back to help, but what good would that do?

Peggy's voice was weak, her throat constricted by fear. Her shout was little more than a croak. 'Run!' she screamed. 'Run!'

At the sound of his sister's voice a rush of adrenaline-filled Robert's veins. He knew he had to keep her safe – keep them all safe - and standing alone he felt powerful and in control of the situation. He saw Maude away to his right and his sister in open space a little further out. The professor was closing in on them and Robert only hoped the others would be able to escape. He had to give them more time. He fumbled with the rolled-up needle in his pocket as he willed his father to help him, for the others get away, then opened his arms and stood his ground. 'You want me?' he called. 'I'm here! Come and get me!'

Professor Barnforth changed direction. 'Don't let him get away.' The dark-haired man raised a hand in acknowledgement and started towards Robert, leaving Will free to circle towards the girls.

Will's breath was ragged as much from fear as from exertion. He couldn't believe his eyes as his friend stood his ground. 'What's he doing?'

Peggy saw things differently and grinned. 'He's giving us the chance to escape,' she said, and gave a nervous half-laugh, knowing her brother and hoping she was right. 'To him, it's a huge game of tig, and no one ever catches Robert at tig. Everyone wants him on their team when we play back at home because he's just too fast. He's uncatchable. Trust me, he has no intention of being caught.'

Robert led the men adance. Wherever they went, he countered by moving in the opposite direction, his movements calculated and strategic like a game of cat and mouse. And he did it all with an amused smile upon his face.

The men followed as Robert circled back and forth, using the headstones to his advantage. The blonde-haired man came to a halt a few feet before Robert. He was panting heavily, the exertion causing him to sweat in the heat of the day, but Robert stood calmly with his back to one of the stone crosses. The man assumed Robert was trapped.

'Where you go now, little boy?' The words were mismatched, his vowels slightly forced like a false accent. The man did not sound fluent in the English language.

Robert smirked. 'I'm not the one doing the running, mister,' he said, then took a step sideways and moved backwards into the dense cover of the trees.

The man rolled his eyes in exasperation and stood with his hands on his hips as he considered his next move. *He's a child. How difficult can he be to catch?*

Robert vanished between the trunks, but as he hid, his pursuer made a split-second decision and dashed diagonally forwards. Where he expected to find Robert he discovered empty space, and Robert slipped behind the trunk of two more trees that grew so close together they were almost one.

The man ran a hand through his hair and stood listening for the slightest sound. He heard nothing. Where had the boy gone? The blonde-haired man circled the area where he had assumed Robert to be standing, but when he dashed forwards Robert was nowhere to be seen. The man turned a slow circle, his anger building. 'I will find you,' he called. 'You cannot hide forever.'

Robert had always enjoyed hide and seek, and at that moment he was in command of the game. He watched the man through a slither of a gap between the trees and smiled. The man took quick strides, hoping to flush Robert out, but the grass between the roots made Robert's movements silent and he was able to slip behind the man undetected. He dropped to a low crouch behind the trunk of a fallen tree as the Professor entered the woodland.

The Professor circled in one direction, the blonde-haired man in the opposite. They hoped to sweep the boy into view but Robert wasn't about to be caught out. He picked up a stone and threw it into the canopy. The noise caused both men to look up and he threw another stone in the opposite direction, watching from the cover of a low branch long enough to see the men studying the tree tops. While they were distracted he moved towards the wall that ran along the edge of the churchyard, but with his attention focused upon the men before him, he had not seen the bespectacled man circle around and enter the tree line from behind.

Robert slipped from tree to tree, his body shielded amongst the woodland growth as Professor Barnforth and his associate scoured the area away to the right. He trod silently, every move measured, every footstep careful, but doing so put him closer to the figure on the tree line, and he had no idea the man was there.

Will and the girls saw Robert step out of the shadows. They also saw the figure of the bespectacled man shadowing him along the edge of the trees. The man's steps were slow and silent, and Peggy let out a yell as the figure crept into the wood, causing Robert to look around. The man froze, his body crouched in secrecy, his foot mid-step upon a twig made brittle by the summer warmth. The twig snapped, the sound loud in the silence, and Robert's eyes flicked to the man standing directly behind him. Their eyes locked.

The blonde-haired man pushed his glasses up his nose and folded his arms. 'You have no way escape,' he said, his polite English voice replaced by a foreign accent and missing vocabulary. Robert was too busy looking around to pay any attention. He watched as the Professor and the bespectacled man moved in behind him, then made a sudden dash to the wall on his right. He used the element of surprise to scale the wall, his feet finding purchase on its stony construction.

Just as he was about to drop into the freedom beyond, a hand grabbed him by the ankle and pulled. Robert twisted, kicked out with his other foot and caught the bespectacled man on the chin. The German grunted but gave another pull and Robert found himself at the base of the wall.

A vision of his father, stripped to his vest and trousers, braces hanging at his sides and his fists raised in a boxing pose, flashed before him. He remembered how his father had taught him to fight and scrambled to his feet, fists raised, knuckles white, his fingers nipped tightly into the palms of his hands. He wasn't about to make it easy for them.

'Oh-ho! Little man wants to fight with the big boys!' mocked the German. He crouched before Robert, his fists raised in mimicry, but instantly regretted it as Robert punched him hard in the mouth. *You need to know how to defend,* his father had taught him, *but also how to attack. Make the first blow count because shock is an important tactic.*

The bespectacled man recoiled, surprised that the boy had actually struck him, and doubly shocked at the ferocity of it. He paused, initially unsure how to respond towards a child, but when Robert punched again he was prepared and pushed the boy hard in the chest. Robert fell backwards and the German raised the back of his hand as though to cuff Robert around the head. 'Enough!' he snarled, 'or I show you proper discipline. German discipline!'

Robert did not flinch, his body ready to take the slap, but instead of following through with the punishment, the bespectacled man made a decision about how things would be from that moment on. He pulled a pistol from under his jacket and waved it at Robert. 'Enough,' he repeated.

The blonde-haired man had seen the entire exchange and laughed. 'Bested by de kinder, eh, Karl?' He grinned. 'What would our friends in the Fatherland think of that,   I wonder?'

Karl turned, the gun still in his hand. The relationship between the two men was not good and Karl had little time or patience for the other man. He was often told he was too single-minded and not prepared to consider others, but on this occasion, he put the gun away. The child had seen it. Perhaps the sight of it would be enough.

A glimmer of hope settled the unease Robert had felt. Perhaps he would not be treated too harshly after all, but he remained guarded and ready to defend himself nevertheless. He climbed to his feet and stood ready, his feet apart and his weight balanced as he watched for the slightest opportunity. His father had taught him well and he was not above exploiting the slightest weakness. He had already dented one German's pride and was prepared to do it again.

'Both of you, calm yourselves.' The professor waved the two men away. He glanced at Karl's bloodied face and then turned to Robert. 'You did that?' he said. 'Well done! You have spirit, but lower your fists. There is no need for further aggression.'

A wry smile crossed the Professor's face as he turned back towards Karl. 'When we have finished here, perhaps the boy can give you some lessons?' He raised his eyebrows in amusement, but Karl did not respond. The bespectacled man sniggered and Professor Barnforth turned on him. 'And you, Jakob, keep watch. We have been seen once too often today.'

The Professor returned his attention to Robert. 'We have no desire to hurt you, but that is up to you. We were just surprised to have you listening to our conversation, and we did not think it appropriate.' He reached out and attempted to straighten Robert's jumper, but Robert batted the hand away. 'Did your parents not teach you it was rude to eavesdrop?'

Robert's eyes darted between the men, Karl scowling at Robert as he dabbed at his lip with a pocket handkerchief. Robert smirked, but Professor Barnforth placed a finger beneath his chin and turned his face towards him. Robert pushed the hand away once more. 'Don't touch me,' he hissed.

The Professor studied the boy before him. 'Two of your friends I recognise, but you and the girl I do not. Tell me, are you the evacuees I've been hearing about?' Robert remained silent. The Professor continued. 'With that kind of fire, I can only assume you are the little thug who thought it appropriate to kick my wife.' He searched for a name. 'Robert, I believe you are called.' He leaned forwards, hands upon his knees. 'You are quite the little tearaway from what I hear, but your sister - ' he screwed up his mouth, 'I'm afraid her name eludes me.'

Robert's eyes flared. He was not about to give up her name, and instead shuffled into a better position to make a run for it. The Professor pushed him gently back. 'Ah-ah, I do not think so. Now tell me – and please think very carefully about this – what did you hear?'

When Robert did not speak, Professor Barnforth reached out and grabbed Robert by the ear. He twisted it enough to cause pain but not enough for Robert to cry out. 'Now, Robert,' he twisted again but Robert continued to hold back, 'I urge you to think a little bit harder. You would not like it if we had to persuade you further.'

Will moved silently towards the tree line. He held his breath and listened as voices mumbled just beyond his hearing, but needn't have bothered. Robert's cry was sharp and clear, and Will knew instantly his friend was in trouble. But what could he do on his own against three men? The last thing he wanted was for the girls to become involved. He was prepared to shoulder the pain of being hurt, but Mother would be terribly cross if he allowed anything to happen to Peggy or his sister.

A branch the thickness of his wrist lay to his right. It was about four feet long and divided into a sturdy-looking fork that split into further branches and twigs. He hefted it in both hands and felt confident he could wield it with some power.

Will prepared himself. Normally he wasn't one to cause trouble, if the men really were Germans, then he was defending his friends, his village, and his country. It was his Civic Duty - Captain Reed had told them so – and it was only right that he stand up to them. He felt nervous but was prepared to do whatever he must.

He hefted the branch. It felt good in his hands and he held it across his chest the way he had seen the Home Guard hold their rifles.

A sound caused him to turn. Peggy and Maude stood behind him, their pockets bulging with stones, the largest they could find gripped in each hand. Peggy tossed one and caught it confidently. 'That's my brother,' she said firmly. 'You coming?'

The grass cushioned their approach. It wasn't until they were almost upon them that Karl sensed they were no longer alone. He half-turned in time to glimpse the branch as it was thrust into his face. It knocked him sideways and his glasses flew into the undergrowth. Blood gushed from his nose.

Peggy launched the largest of her stones from almost point-blank range. It caught the professor directly between the shoulder blades, the pain sudden and intense like falling onto a blunt object, and he struggled to suck air into his lungs.

For a few moments he was unable to move and Robert used the professor's pain and disorientation to his advantage. He kicked out, caught the professor in the chest with the flat of his foot and knocked him backwards. Robert was quick to his feet and he moved into open ground.

While a hard impact to the side of the head sent Jakob to his knees, Karl was more resilient. He tried to rise, but Will stabbed him with the broken end of the branch before whipping it over to strike him again with the splayed end. The thicker Y-shaped branches scratched and scraped around his face and neck and he grabbed angrily at them, but Will still had a two-handed hold. He thrust the branch forwards once more, corkscrewing it painfully across Karl's face and catching him in the eyes. Karl turned his face and pressed the heel of his hand to his injured face as he fumbled around for his spectacles. When at last he sat them on his face the bend in their frame caused them to sit awkwardly. He winced as they dug into what felt like a broken nose.

The rescue mission, carried out with a fallen branch and a pocketful of stones, had taken no more than fifteen seconds and had brought all three men to their knees. It was a lesson in the dangers of overconfidence, and a painful one at that.

Will stood with his friends, Robert hefting a stone in his right hand in case he should need it, but slipped it into his pocket and resorted to mockery instead. 'If you are the best Hitler can send, tell him not to bother,' he teased. 'Tell him he hasn't got a chance.'

'Do you really think so?' Karl snarled. 'You Britishers think you are so superior, with your old man's army and your toy Spitfires, but the Fatherland is coming for you, and sooner than you think. We'll see how confident you feel then, shall we?'

A hand suddenly grabbed Robert by the ankle and he kicked out to free himself, but when his kicks had no effect he stamped down hard on Karl's bandaged hand. The German's grip faltered and Robert dug in the heel of his shoe, grinding it into the bones of the man's injured hand. The German released his grip and rolled onto his side as he pulled the injured hand towards him. He groaned in pain and glared at the boy.

The weapon was barely out of Karl's jacket when Peggy's stone hit him hard on the forehead. The sound of its impact was as heavy as it was painful, and blood flowed from the new wound. Karl's consciousness faltered, his gun hand hovering aimlessly, and Will kicked out at it. The gun skittered into the long grass and vanished.

Jakob crept forward, ready to end the stand-off and take back control, but uncertainty plagued him. While he wasn't prepared to use a weapon on children as Karl had been, he found himself in a situation where commitment to the mission and his fatherly instincts were at odds. His eyes wavered between the children and he saw his son standing amongst them, his hair glinting in the sun as it caught the breeze. He considered what his world had come to when he would willingly put the lives of children at risk for the sake of the Nazi Party. Was that really the man he had become?

The sound of engines caught Will's attention. He glanced up through a gap in the trees as another dogfight sketched patterns across the sky. A German aircraft spiralled down from the heavens in a pillar of flame, its giant letter S both horrific and mesmerising in equal measure. He pointed to the battle overhead. 'Not going so well today, is it?'

'We will see,' Karl struggled to his feet, doubly angered by Jakob's weakness. He made a sudden grab for the children, but by the time the girls had launched their stones it was too late. Maude was caught off-guard and her aim went wild. Peggy's was a weak effort.

Robert found himself hauled from his feet and thrust against a tree. 'You not go home to mother today,' Karl hissed, and Robert felt his body flush with a hot jolt of fear. He struggled against Karl's grip but quickly realised the man was too strong for him.

'Get off me!' Robert's voice was loud in the stillness. Surely someone would hear and come to investigate, but there was no intervening shout, no offer of help, and he realised he was on his own. He shouted again, his voice rising in pitch. 'Georroff! Leave go!' With only his fists to use as a weapon, he punched at the German's face the way his father had taught him, but his struggle was futile.

Somehow, Robert found the stone in his hand. He did not recall reaching into his pocket, but he brought it down hard. Its rough edges cut into the flesh of Karl's nose as he hammered at the frame of the German's glasses. Karl grunted, pain spiking into his face and eyes and blood flowed from a fresh wound that had opened up, yet still, Karl maintained his grip. Robert was trapped.

The stone shifted in his fingers, its surface slick with a film of blood and he gripped at it, desperate not to let it slip away, and then it was gone. He watched in horror as the stone fell, bounced off his knee and vanished amongst the long grass. A cry of desperation welled up, thin and wailing at first, before anger took hold and it became a scream of rage.

He clawed at the face before him, his fingers scratching and his thumbs digging into the man's eyes in an attempt to force his release, but Karl screwed up his eyes and mouth and turned his face away. He growled at Robert, his words gruff and short as he spat them, and when Robert continued he felt himself slammed against a tree with enough force to knock the wind from his lungs.

Pain flared inside his head and his vision wavered, his brain filled with a fuzz of disorientation, but when the fog began to clear he realised Karl had set him down. Whether because of the pain Robert had inflicted or for some other reason, he did not know, but Robert felt solid ground beneath his feet and sensed he had the advantage.

The last thing Karl expected was another fight, but that was precisely what Robert gave him. In those first vital seconds, something sparked within him, an inescapable sense of purpose, and he understood he was about to make a difference that would radiate like ripples across a pond. A thin smile creased one corner of his mouth.

Karl looked quizzically as Robert's face took on an all-knowing look. It was an expression of confidence unfitting for the situation, and Karl didn't know whether it was simple arrogance, boyish bluster, or whether the boy knew something that was about to unravel their carefully laid plans. It concerned him, and for the first time, Karl considered his position.

He was not prepared to be bettered by a child, his arrogant belief in German superiority a thread that ran through every part of his being, but there was something about this child that made him wary. Karl still believed he had the upper hand, but when Robert's grin widened he saw strength and cunning in the boy's eyes. Too late, he realised he had been outwitted.

Robert's knee came up so hard and fast into Karl's groin that he had not even considered such an action. It caught him off guard and overwhelmed him, his face red, his breath sucked from his lungs by a fierce pain that ached and burned in the pit of his stomach. It felt as though his intestines had been skewered by a red-hot poker and he sagged to the floor, his legs pulled up to his stomach as he struggled to breathe.

Robert stepped back, mindful that both the professor and Jakob were close by, but the professor looked in no state to challenge him and Jakob simply appeared unwilling. He was about to turn and run when something drew his eye. It was the journal, the book that had been passed between the men in St. Thomas' churchyard, the same book that had presumably been stolen from Professor Barnforth's study. Robert realised its importance. It was central to everything that was going on and could no doubt explain much. He took a tentative step forwards and lunged for the journal.

It did not come away on the first attempt, but on the second it slipped free, its leather cover smooth and cool in his hand. Robert moved away quickly, unwilling to stay within grasping distance for longer than necessary – he didn't trust Karl, even if he did appear to be incapacitated - and stumbled over something in the grass. The pistol lay like a prized archaeological find, proof of the German presence in Ravenscroft and the danger they posed. He grabbed it.

With the journal in one hand and the pistol in the other, Robert looked down at the fallen Germans. 'Thank you for these,' he said, raising the items in both hands, 'but I'll take them if you don't mind. I think the Home Guard will be very interested when we tell them what you've been up to.' And with that, he turned and ran.

The gun felt heavy in Robert's hand, its metal cold against his palm. The possibility the weapon might go off filled him with fear but he dare not slow down, the gun, the journal and the knowledge there were Germans in Ravenscroft too important to keep between them.

The boys kept pace with one another, but Robert kept glancing over his shoulder, terrified that Karl or Jakob or Professor Barnforth would suddenly be there, hands outstretched to pull him to the ground and take back what was theirs, but he only saw Peggy and Maude. The girls slipped behind and he eased his pace as they shouted for him to slow down.

Will took hold of Robert's arm and lifted it. 'Let's see.' He reached out for the gun but Robert held it away from him. 'Come on, pass it 'ere. Let's have hold.'

Robert kept it out of reach. He didn't even know if it was loaded. Will tried again. 'Come on, let's see - ' He was put out that Robert wouldn't share the weapon, but it was dangerous and Robert felt the weight of responsibility.

'It's not a toy!' snapped Robert, his tone irritated. Will was his friend but there were some lines that even friends didn't cross, and this was one of them.

Peggy and Maude ambled to a halt, their legs tired from the exertion. Will was still making noises about holding the gun but the girls sided with Robert. 'Mother wouldn't let you,' said Maude. 'It be dangerous.' Will frowned but his sulk went unnoticed.

Wrapping the gun in his jumper, Robert tucked it under his arm. 'Come on, we have to get this to the Home Guard. They'll know what to do with it,' he said. 'They'll want to know about the Germans too. They're soldiers. It's their job.'

Chapter 12

The children asked to speak to Captain Reed in private and he took them into the back room of his butcher's shop. His coat and trilby hung from the back of the door, his gas mask atop them amid boxes of shop goods and the machinery for mincing meat and making sausages.

'And what is so important that you insist I come away from my customers?' Captain Reed was busy and not happy at the interruption, but when Robert placed his jumper on the table and unrolled it to reveal a Luger, the pistol of choice with German forces, he understood.

Relieved to see the safety catch was in the locked position, he unloaded the pistol, placed the gun carefully inside a drawer and locked it. He dropped the bullets into his trouser pocket and patted them subconsciously.

'Now,' he said gently, not wanting to be authoritative, but needing to know exactly what had gone on, 'the obvious question is, where on earth did you find that?'

The children all spoke at once and the captain held up his hands. 'Whoa! Steady on, now.' The children's voices trailed off. 'I can't listen to you all at once.' He pointed a finger at Robert. 'Young man, tell me how you came across such a thing.'

Robert swallowed. This should have been easy, but it wasn't. After everything that had happened in recent weeks, it seemed his brushes with authority had become more common. He began to wonder whether he had gained the wrong kind of reputation.

What if they weren't believed? What if Captain Reed thought they were simply making it all up? But he had just handed over a pistol - a German pistol – and he swallowed again. 'From a spy,' he said at last. 'A German spy.'

The captain folded his arms. *As if a German pilot isn't enough to be going on with,*.and then remembered the barbed wire and the lights the children had reported a few days ago. 'Here, in Ravenscroft?'

The children answered with a combination of nods and polite *Yes, Sirs*. 'And we have this,' said Peggy, her voice timid as she laid the journal next to Robert's jumper. 'It's Professor Barnforth's.'

Captain Reed raised his eyebrows. 'Professor Barnforth's?' He turned the journal over in his hands and unfastened the leather strap that bound the book closed. Inside were neatly written notes and intricate diagrams, the penmanship detailed and precise, as though made by a person who took great pride in their work. 'You do know a journal like this was stolen from Professor Barnforth's study this morning?'

'It wasn't us.' Robert was eager to defend his friends. 'That's the truth.'

Reed peered at Robert as though assessing him. He waved the boy's worries to silence. 'I believe you,' he said. He flicked a few more pages. 'But I feel sure the professor will be glad to have this returned to him. After all, it's - '

'Professor Barnforth were there as well. With the Germans,' added Maude. She didn't like to interrupt, having been taught to wait for a pause before speaking, but the current situation did not seem to fit.

Peggy nodded. 'He was speaking with them – '

'Them?' The captain was alarmed by the prospect of more than one German infiltrator in the village.

Maude nodded. 'There were two,' she said. 'It were as if Professor Barnforth knew both men.' She indicated the journal. 'They passed book around an' professor showed Germans somethin' inside it. 'e knew where to look.'

'And they called him Herr Barnforth,' said Will. 'Said somethin' bout Führer and – '

'Can you remember precisely what?'

Will thought for a moment. 'About not forgetting.'

' "The Führer will not forget this," ' quoted Robert.

Will nodded. 'That were it.'

'Did they say anything else? The smallest detail could be of the utmost importance here. Take your time. Think carefully.'

'Somethin' bout relics,' added Maude. 'Don't know what it means though.'

'And where was this?' the captain asked.

'In cemetery at St. Thomas'. We was cuttin' through to stepping-stones when we 'eard voices. They were behind church when we saw Professor Barnforth. We hid between gravestones to listen.' Maude instantly regretted being so open. 'Please don't tell Mother we was listening,' she said. 'we'll be in awful trouble.'

Captain Reed smiled. 'In this case, you should have no concerns,' he said gently. 'This is of great importance, and I believe your mother would be more than willing to overlook such a small indiscretion in the circumstances.' He nipped at the end of his nose. 'But I have to ask, beyond what you have told me, what made you think the men were German?'

'Because they told us,' said Robert. 'They chased us once they knew we'd heard them.'

'That's how we ended up with the gun and the journal,' added Peggy. 'Robert grabbed both when he got away.'

The captain studied the children for a moment. 'Wait here.' He ducked back into the shop. Voices faded as customers left and he flipped the sign on the door to CLOSED before returning to the back room.

'I've sent a message to assemble the Home Guard,' he said. 'In the meantime – ' He pulled out a chair and motioned for the children to do the same, then took a notebook and pencil stub from his pocket and laid them on the tabletop.

'Right,' he said, looking at them all in turn. 'Let's start at the beginning. We don't want to miss anything, now do we?'

*   *   *

Betty didn't know whether to be upset the children had been through such an ordeal, annoyed they had put themselves in such danger to begin with, or proud of the mature way in which they had handled themselves. She opted for somewhere between all three.

If she was honest with herself, she was a little concerned at Robert's bravado and his willingness to confront such men. Suppose they had been shot? The thought left her cold.

'You best keep out of it from now on,' she instructed. 'Home Guard have job to do, so you leave 'em be. Last thing they want is children int way.' She finished stirring a pot of soup she had on the stove and tapped the spoon on the edge of the saucepan before wiping her hands on a towel. 'Anyways, you've been lax over past few days. Animals won't look after the'selves, so go finish up your chores,' she said, then made a firm addition: 'But mind you stay within farm boundary. My stomach be awhirl as it is.'

Maude spoke for herself and Peggy when she said they would, but wasn't so sure about the boys. Her brother was easily led, and she had a sneaking suspicion Robert had become a bad influence upon him of late. She didn't know how Mother would react if the boys involved themselves in anything else.

* * *

Robert and Will straddled a fence rail as they fired pebbles from a catapult at a target they had erected on top of a fencepost. Robert had a better aim than Will and had hit the target twice so far. It seemed he possessed a natural ability with such things.

'Do you miss home?' Betty had told both Will and Maude to avoid asking in case it caused any upset, making Will's question unexpected: *You must be mindful o' people's feelings*, Betty had told him. *How would you feel if you were taken from 'ome and put wi' someone you'd not met before?* Will had heeded that advice, but the question came out without him thinking about it.

Robert pursed his lips as he remembered the inside of his home. It was a small mid-terraced house with two bedrooms upstairs, a living room and small kitchen downstairs, and a lavatory in the yard next to the coal shed. A tin bath hung from a nail alongside a metal tub and dolly-peg used on wash day. Inside, the rooms were sparsely furnished with second-hand but well-loved furniture, the carpets tattered and thread-bare in places and strewn with clippy mats. Mother and Father had not been well-off and had struggled to make ends meet, but had always done their best to provide for their children. They had often gone without themselves as a result, but it was not something they would have admitted to.

Robert nodded and looked up. 'I do,' he said, after a pause. His voice was quiet, his thoughts somewhere distant. 'I miss mother and father a lot.' He shifted position on the fence rail, its discomfort a welcome distraction. 'Feels like father's been away forever. I miss him too, but I'm sort of used to that.'

'I never knew my father,' said Will. He looked sideways at Robert. 'My real father, I mean.' He jumped down and balanced his left wrist on the fence as he pulled the elastic back with his right hand and took aim. He poked his tongue from the corner of his mouth in concentration. When he missed the target he tucked the catapult into the pocket of his shorts and leaned against the fence. The ground was uneven, the grass growing in clumps that sprouted long fronds of meadow grass, and he began toeing at it absentmindedly. 'Mother don't think I know Ken not be my father,' he added. 'He's always lived wi' us, though. Treats us well, he does. Best father we could've 'ad.'

'What about Maude? Is she – ?'

Will nodded. 'She's theirs, but not Phillip.'

Robert frowned and Will waved an hand, the gesture suggesting it was a bit of a tale. 'He really be my cousin, but it be complicated. Mother's sister an' 'usband were killed 'bout six year ago. Bus ran off road and crashed into shelter they was standin' in. Killed 'em both, so Phillip came to us. That's one reason Mrs Barnforth don't like us much. Says we're not proper family. Says we don't belong in village. That an fact mother weren't married when I were born. Mother don't think I knows bout that, though.'

Robert nodded. 'She doesn't like me either. Or Peggy.' He wrinkled his nose. 'Don't like her anyway, so that makes us even.' He jumped down and they walked towards the head of the field where a gate stood open.

'I see postman brought another letter,' said Will.

Robert nodded but remained silent. The letter had been filled with news of what had happened to their friends and neighbours, and how a stray bomb had come down in the middle of Highfield Road, narrowly missing the milk woman who had been caught in the open by the unexpected raid. The bomb had turned out to be a dud but had buried itself under six feet of earth and rubble, startling the milk woman's horse and tipping the cart over. The neighbourhood had been left without their milk ration that day, much to the annoyance of all. Beyond that, Mother had said little about herself. It was as though she had avoided the subject deliberately.

'Didn't say much,' said Robert. 'Mother said she's well, but hasn't heard from father. That was it.' He shrugged, being only partly truthful and moved to the gate. He pulled it closed, raising his eyes to the sky as a distant siren began its terrifying wail. It rooted the boys to the spot.

The air began to drone, a low, discordant sound that vibrated from every direction yet appeared to originate from nowhere. It increased to a pulsating voice against the silence of the day, and across the horizon, a staggered line of dots appeared. They grew in size until the boys could pick out individual aircraft, bombers moving south along the coastline in search of targets. Their formation was followed by another line that banked inland.

Fire and death exploded across the sky, anti-aircraft shells leaving imprints upon the heavens like flowering ink upon damp paper. Lethal fragments of shrapnel cut through the air with devastating effect and one of the bombers' engines began to smoke. It coughed and died, and the aircraft struggled to stay aloft as it peeled away on a course for home. Another took a dead-hit and exploded mid-flight, its remains tumbling earthward. Mercifully its bombs fell with it to detonate across the empty fields below.

Enemy fighters darted between the anti-aircraft explosions like angry hornets, their pilots put to the test as the guns pummeled the sky around them, and then the gunfire ceased.

Spitfires and Hurricanes dropped on the approaching bombers, raking them with heavy cannon fire. Several sustained damage but somehow maintained their course and height as the German escort fighters threw themselves upon the British pilots. They spiralled, the RAF defending, the Luftwaffe attempting to press on with their attack as bombs dropped, the air whistling and screaming as they fell. The boys watched in horror as destruction rained down upon Whitby.

The ground beneath their feet rumbled, each detonation sending up a plume of smoke that hung like an evil spirit freed from captivity. It was a sight neither boy had witnessed before and was something they would never forget.

Naval vessels moored within Whitby's harbour walls came under attack and the ships bared their teeth in defiance. The lead bomber took heavy fire and pitched seawards, smoke and flame trailing behind it as the pilot struggled to control its plunge towards the ocean. The end was inevitable.

With attention focused on the main assault, a solitary aircraft peeled away. Its escort fighters held back from the main fight, banking away from the coastline as the aircraft headed inland, and kept formation with it. There would be time later to join the cutting edge of the raid, but for now, they had other orders. Their mission must not fail.

The boys watched in stunned silence as the aircraft circled over the village and headed north. Streamers fell from it one after the other, fluttering momentarily before filling with air and billowing open to drift behind the aircraft. The sight was mesmerising, its meaning terrifying.

'Paratroopers!' croaked Will. His words caught in his throat, the implications all too real. Was this it, the first step in the German invasion of Britain?

Robert stood alongside his friend in stunned silence. He did not know whether to be frightened or angry at the sight, then an iron fist of determination filled his stomach and he vowed to do whatever he needed to when the time arose.

The *tat-tat-tat* of gunfire reached them upon the summer air as brave Spitfire pilots chased the escort fighters down and Hurricanes tackled the bombers. Planes fell from the sky; whether British or German, it was not always possible to tell, yet everything about the raid was a spectacle. Standing beneath it, as they counted the descending parachutes, Robert suddenly felt very small

'Eighteen,' said Will. He watched their trail expand across the sky until the first paratrooper hit the hillside. His canopy fluttered before collapsing, the remaining parachutes mere seconds behind. 'Carrion's Wood,' he said. 'They've landed by Carrion's Wood, but eighteen? Surely that not be enough to invade. What can they 'ope to do wi' just eighteen men?'

Robert had one foot on the fence. 'Let's go and see.' He had the beginnings of a smile on his face, the same look he had given in the churchyard as he dodged between the headstones. It had felt the right thing to do then and he felt the same now, empowered to do something in the defence of Ravenscroft, the place he had begun to think of as home. He had made such a personal vow only minutes before and was prepared to act upon it now.

Will shook his head. 'No way! It's not just a few men we can give run-around to like before int graveyard. They're proper soldiers. German soldiers. They have guns an' grenades an' the like. What good we be 'gainst that?'

'But that's just the point,' said Robert. 'There's nobody between us and them, so it's up to us. We're British and this is our country, so if I can do something to help stop them, I'm doing it. Don't matter how dangerous it is. Don't matter we're only kids, but my father, yours, those pilots up there are fighting to stay alive, fighting to beat the Germans back. If they can do it, then so can we.'

Will watched the final parachutes deflate as the soldiers hit the ground. Only the drone of engines as the aircraft battled above their heads gave any indication anything that something was unfolding.

'Anyway, last thing they'll expect is kids to show up,' said Robert. 'They won't shoot us, it would be like shooting at their own. Even Germans can't be that bad.'

'That's what we thought about Karl,' grumbled Will.

'Yeah, well you'd be mad if you got beaten up by a bunch of kids,' added Robert, grinning. 'Especially a couple of girls.' He jumped down on the far side of the fence. 'Come on, let's see what's happening. We don't have time to waste.'

*   *   *

The attack brought the village to a standstill. Where the war had scarcely touched Ravenscroft so far, this raid was on their doorstep and it brought with it the reality that friends and relatives were suffering. Many stood with their faces to the sky, searching, willing, praying for victory and the safety of their own.

A parachute appeared as a pilot bailed out, his canopy blossoming like a flower. Another aircraft followed, the scene changing from moment to moment as fighters darted and tested one another, courage and nerves of steel the ultimate victor.

Betty watched, a fist of unease tightening in her stomach as a German bomber broke free. It circled towards the village and a Spitfire dived upon it. Two Messerschmitts turned to meet the attack, their guns hammering, and the Spitfire retreated to loop high above and drop in from a fresh angle of attack. Even to Betty's untrained eye, something about the scene appeared wrong.

Why were the fighters protecting a lone aircraft? What did they hope to achieve? There was nothing of importance in the fields surrounding Ravenscroft for them to target, so why were they heading inland? Even the anti-aircraft guns that protected the coast were embedded on East Cliff overlooking Whitby.

The girls pressed up against Betty as they watched, their arms around her waist, but Phillip remained a step away. Since their father had been called up, Phillip had taken on the role of man-of-the-house. He acted as though he was too old for such affection, at least in front of his younger siblings.

Betty's head and heart battled for control, her worry at the boys' whereabouts foremost in her mind, and anxiety gripped her stomach like an ever-tightening band. She chewed at her lip, the scene above eating into her soul as she prayed for their safety.

The enemy bomber circled, its course bringing it closer to the village while fighters buzzed angrily around it. Did they have orders to attack the villages beyond the fringe of Whitby, or was this something more, some nightmare that would change their lives forever?

A hand slid into hers and Betty gripped it tightly, a wave of panic flowing through her as the aircraft approached. A silent scream lodged in her throat and she fought to force it down, to remain composed and in control in front of the girls, but the fear of being separated from her family was laid bare. She ushered the girls towards the Anderson shelter dug into the garden alongside the house. It had stood empty so far, its atmosphere damp and earthen-smelling, but now was the time to make use of it.

With the girls safely inside Betty raised a hand to watch the aircraft. Her blood froze as it completed its turn and headed north in the direction of Carrion's Wood, a trail of parachutes behind it like dandelion seeds adrift upon the wind.

Chapter 13

Captain Reed wiped the sweat from his brow. His attention had been drawn from leading the search for Professor Barnforth and his accomplices to the aircraft that now circled overhead. He was aware the Home Guard presented the first line of defence, but this was not what he had been expecting.

Agitation rippled through the men like unease before a storm. By their own admission, they were a rag-tag group of men too old or not fit enough to fight, with only a few who had fought in the Great War having any kind of training at all. Their numbers had been swollen by local men who had volunteered to join the search, but with a handful of rifles and too few bullets between them, what possible defence could they hope to achieve if it came to a confrontation?

Voices shouted against the sound of the aircraft as they swung overhead. Messerschmitts buzzed low to the ground and forced the men to run for cover, the hedges and trees that bordered the field offering scant protection. Those with rifles took aim, their throats dry, their hands as steady as they could manage, but they knew there was little they could do.

The Fatherland is coming for you.

Sooner than you think.

Talking to the children he had been sceptical such a bold claim was anything more than German arrogance, but now he wasn't so sure. He considered the possibility there had been intent within their words after all.

He looked up in time to witness the first parachutes stream from the side hatch of the German aircraft. Canopies fluttered momentarily, then billowed open as they descended towards the hilltop and Carrion's Wood. Tension gripped him like a fist. *So, this is it*, he thought. *Invasion.*

The pistol felt leaden in his hand. *What good is this going to be against a platoon of German paratroopers?* He had six bullets in the chamber and another six in a small leather pouch on his belt, hardly enough to dent a division of fully-equipped paratroopers. *But I have to try*, he told himself, realising the ridiculousness of such a belief. There was every probability he would be dead within the first exchange of gunfire or injured at the very least. *We should withdraw and set up a perimeter to defend the village. It's the most sensible course of action.*

He beckoned the senior men together. 'We have to assume this is an advance party with more drops to follow, so we need to be ready,' he said. He turned to his First Lieutenant. 'Bill, I want the men in pairs with a weapon in each group. Position them at every road junction, every pathway and farm track into the village from the north. Keep a clear line of sight from group to group and have the men be ready to offer support at any point of enemy incursion.'

Bill Taylor nodded, the life-long friendship between them put to the side for the moment, the professional needs of the situation coming to the fore. 'Sir.'

Reed turned to his second Lieutenant. 'Stan, take two men and establish a lookout position, somewhere high. The steeple on St. Thomas' should give you a good all-round view. We need to know what the enemy is doing, but keep the men out of sight. There is every chance of sniper fire and we don't want to lose anyone.' He looked between both men. 'Clear?'

Nods all around.

'Right. Get to it.'

*   *   *

Robert and Will hugged the hedgerow as they worked their way around the edge of the field. They crossed two areas of open grassland, staying low to the ground as they approached Monks', Hill where a copse of trees bordered the adjoining field. A stream had carved out a narrow ditch to one side and they stopped to take a drink, the warm day and their nerves having made them thirsty.

Will sifted stones and pocketed a few while they rested. It was an unconscious action, but once he realised what he had done he reasoned they could very well come in handy.

The boys were determined to remain out of sight. While they knew the general direction the parachutes had come down they had no idea exactly where the men had landed, and did not wish to be mistaken for a target. The consequences of venturing forward were troubling enough, but the true danger would likely present itself later.

Will dropped a final stone into his pocket – one for luck, he told himself – and peered up at the tree line. 'Might be a good place to watch from,' said Robert. 'Trees look thicker there.' He set off at a pace and Will followed, the stones heavy, their weight comforting, and he pushed the catapult deeper into his pocket. Its presence felt reassuring.

Reaching the line of trees, Robert dropped to the ground and scrambled the final few feet into the undergrowth. Will crawled in behind him and together they shuffled around in search of a view of the field beyond. A fork in the low branches offered Will a partial view.

Carrion's Wood ran lengthwise across the field opposite, their position placing them at its south-western corner. 'Can you see anything?' Will's voice was scarcely above a whisper, yet his words sounded loud in the stillness.

Robert shook his head and shuffled position slightly. He peered through another gap in the branches, not sure whether he had seen something move against the edge of the wood, and without taking his eyes from the gap in the branches he reached out and tapped at Will's shoulder. 'C'mere,' he whispered, and when Will did not respond he tapped again. Still nothing.

The sound of catapult elastic being drawn caught his attention. He frowned as Will leaned forward upon his right knee, the catapult ready to fire, but at what? The field was empty. Surely Will hadn't chosen this moment to conduct a spot of target practise? Robert shifted his weight and leaned in to look along Will's line of sight. A shadow moved on the other side of the trees and Robert froze.

A German paratrooper knelt in the field just beyond their position, his machine gun slung over his shoulder as he upended his boot to empty a stone. It was obvious he had not been alerted to the boys' presence, and Robert's heart jumped into his mouth as he waited to see what would happen next. He swallowed, but the attempt created a cough that struggled to escape and he bit down on it in a futile effort to remain silent. He failed.

The Paratrooper's head snapped around and he grabbed for his rifle, one boot on, one boot off. He pointed his machine gun towards the tree line and took a step forward, peering into the thicket as he attempted to separate shadows from daylight.

Will tracked his target with the catapult, and as Robert bit down upon a second cough, the paratrooper's eyes scanned towards them. His face reacted in alarm as two pairs of eyes peered back at him from the undergrowth, and he turned his machine gun towards them.

Will had never proved himself a particularly good shot, but this one had to count. He held his breath, narrowed his eyes, and released the sling.

In the instant it took the paratrooper to turn his weapon, the stone crossed the distance between them. The force of the impact knocked the German off his feet and he fell backwards, the pain of being struck at such close range excruciating.

Will reloaded and let the catapult go a second time, the stone striking the man on the side of his face. The soldier grunted in pain, his response quickly turning to anger and he scrambled to his knees.

Unable to see properly, the paratrooper's bullets went wild. 'I thought you said he wouldn't shoot us?' cried Will.

The sound of gunfire deafened him and his ears rang with its after-effects.

The paratrooper fumbled a fresh magazine into his weapon and Robert used the valuable seconds to scramble out from his hiding place. He grabbed Will by the arm and hauled him away. 'Go!' he shouted, his voice thin and barely making a sound above the ringing in his ears. 'Run!'

Will took off down the incline and Robert turned to follow, but the paratrooper pushed the muzzle of his weapon through the hedgerow above him and Robert froze. Luckily the undergrowth shielded him from the paratrooper's view, but the muzzle of the weapon was so close Robert could have reached out and grabbed it.

He sunk low to the ground and felt something hard beneath his palm, its shape familiar. He looked down, saw the catapult and realised Will must have dropped it.

Robert groped around in the dirt for a stone but found nothing. His heart sank until his fingers found one about half the size of an egg. He fumbled it into the catapult's sling and lay back in the dirt, the elastic drawn back as far as it would go. His heart thudded in his ears.

As the paratrooper leaned over the hedgerow in search of a target, Robert closed one eye and centred his aim upon the German's exposed neck and chin.

He had one chance. He could not afford to miss.

*   *   *

Will raced back the way they had come. There seemed no point in hugging the hedgerows this time; they had been seen and speed was more important than remaining hidden. He ran faster than he had ever thought possible, his throat tight, his heart thudding in panic. He stumbled once and went sprawling in the long grass, a scream of panic escaping his lips as he scrambled to his feet. His whole body trembled, yet somehow he managed to find his feet and race on.

Robert wasn't so lucky. He set off downhill on legs that felt numb, the paratrooper behind him clawing at his throat as he fought to draw breath. Another paratrooper stepped out of the trees to Robert's right and he changed direction, racing along the incline towards the field boundary with no idea of where he would go from there. 'Father, help me. Please,' he whispered, his voice loud in his head.

A shadow moved swiftly, the branches powerful, the effect upon the German paratrooper swift and final as he was flung through the air like a discarded rag. The soldier landed deep amongst the trees where other branches snatched at him like gnarled fingers fighting over a morsel of food. Cracks opened in their ancient trunks as though to consume him, and the soldier was gone.

Robert ran on in search of escape. The hedgerow was overgrown, offering no way through, and he raced back and forth along its length, searching, desperate, every step tightening the grip of panic around his throat. And where was Will? He had lost sight of him when they separated. Was he safe?

An opening appeared where Robert was sure there had been none before and he squeezed through, branches clawing at his jumper and scratching at his legs, but in seconds he was on the other side and facing Carrion. He froze, unsure what to do. He couldn't go back, that much was certain, but Carrion made the decision for him. 'Come.' He held out an arm. 'I will give you shelter.'

Robert considered his options. Run? Not a good idea, German paratroopers were close by. Hide? He looked around. There was nowhere to go, but Carrion had cared for both him and Will once before, so why shouldn't he trust him now?

The rustle of leaves caught his attention and he glanced around to see the hedgerow filling in behind him, its branches intertwining where he had passed through. It was as though the hedge had parted just to allow him passage, but he knew that could not be. Could it?

'Time is short,' said Carrion. 'Come, I offer safety.' He beckoned Robert forward, the sound of voices behind the hedgerow spurring him into motion, and without thinking, he followed.

Carrion led them towards a thicket where trees and bushes grew as one. A narrow inlet gave way to an open space within where a stone dwelling stood, moss and grass living off its weathered surface as though the entire structure was alive. A single doorway was set into its stonework, the building old and decaying, but it also felt safe. The thicket closed behind them as they passed through, leaving no indication an opening had ever existed.

A simple wooden stool stood by the door and Carrion motioned Robert towards it. 'Sit and rest awhile,' he said, but Robert did not move, the situation causing him to feel uneasy. 'For one so young you have proved yourself with honour against a greater enemy, yet I fear your battle is far from done.'

'This is just the start,' said Robert. 'You do know we're at war with Germany?'

Carrion leaned upon his staff. For a moment he looked tired, but when he spoke his voice held a greater strength than Robert expected. 'These eyes have witnessed many conflicts, but this too will pass,' he said. 'Sadly, the desire to destroy walks hand in hand with hatred, and shows little concern for those affected.' He shook his head. 'It is the way of man.'

'My father is away fighting,' Robert said. His voice wavered as emotion took hold. The old man watched him intently. 'I don't know when I'll see him again.'

'He will never be far, and protect you he will,' said Carrion. 'A good man's spirit always remains with his family.' He paused, and watching Robert intently from beneath bushy eyebrows, added, 'as does yours.' He saw through the boy's pain and did his best to encourage him. 'Rest. Eat. A soldier must keep up his energy if he is to be ready,' he said. When Robert did not move he nudged the stool forward with his staff. 'Sit.'

Robert slid onto the stool, his mind tumbling between a dozen different places and a hundred questions. Carrion plucked an apple from the tree beside Robert, a tree he could have sworn held no fruit only moments before. 'Eat,' Carrion said once again.

The apple tasted delicious, far sweeter than any he had tasted before, and he devoured it quickly. 'That,' he said around a mouthful, indicating the scene beyond the thicket that secluded them. 'The paratrooper, I mean. What happened? Was that you?'

Carrion leaned more heavily upon his staff. He inclined his head to-and-fro as he considered. 'Yes and no.'

Robert nibbled at the remains of the core, his mind awhirl with questions. 'Who are you?'

The old man raised his eyebrows as though pondering a great question. 'History has provided many names, but Carrion seems befitting,' he said, indicating the birds that circled overhead. Their wings were dark against the sunlight.

Robert's next question was a little hesitant, yet bold. 'People say you've been here for hundreds of years. Is that true?'

Carrion shrugged before speaking. 'A fly may occupy its world for thirty days, a man for seventy years, but is each not a full life?' He paused and took stock as though unsure whether to continue, then pressed ahead, his manner serious. 'I was tasked long ago with an oath of responsibility. It is one I have upheld for over a thousand years and will uphold for the next thousand.'

'A thousand years?' Robert thrust his head forwards, his eyes wide in disbelief. The old man's face was lined with rivers of age, his skin weathered and toughened like the oldest of bark, yet Robert could not believe the man before him had lived more than seventy years. To a man of Carrion's life experience, a thousand years was a normal lifetime and he dismissed the boy's question with a wave of the hand. 'Everyone must play a role, some more important than others, but each contributes to this world in their own way.' Now, if you are refreshed?' He indicated the stick that leaned against the wall by the boy's knee.

Like the apple, Robert had not noticed it when he sat down. He looked up quizzically but the old man simply raised his eyebrows and indicated once more with a tilt of the head. 'Come,' he said and stepped back into the centre of the clearing.

The stick was just over two feet long, straight, and stripped of all its bark. One end was slightly thicker so it fit comfortably within the palm of his hand as though moulded, and he tested its weight with a few flicks of the wrist. 'What do you – ' he began, but before he could finish, Carrion's staff lashed out and caught Robert across the knuckles. 'Yeow!' he shouted. 'What was that for?' He dropped the stick and rubbed at his fingers.

Carrion flicked the stick towards Robert with the end of his staff, but when Robert made no move to pick it up he suddenly found himself standing before Carrion in the clearing, the stick in his hand. He had no idea how he came to stand there. 'How - ?' Robert did not have time to finish his question before Carrion's staff flashed out once more, its movement less sudden. Robert instinctively raised the stick to parry the attack, but he was not quick enough and the staff caught him across the back of the hand. He yelped again. 'Why are you doing this?' he cried. 'You said you would defend me, not hurt me.'

'You call yourself King Robert, yet you dither over a few blows,' he said. 'Where is your strength now? Where is your leadership?'

King Robert? He remembered calling himself that while mock sword-fighting with Will at the Tops, but how could the old man have heard? The flutter of wings, their feathers as

127

dark as soot, caught his attention and then he realised: a large black bird had circled while they played. Had Carrion been spying on him? Spying on all of them?

'Our strength and our decisions are the behaviours that define us,' said Carrion, 'and while your deeds today have shown your worth, you must be willing to do more, bruised knuckles or not.'

Robert looked inwards. The challenges he had faced, the physical and emotional pain he had suffered all rose to meet him and he realised Carrion was right. He had sworn to do whatever he could, and it appeared he was being given the skills to do just that.

'Now.' Carrion stepped forward and Robert raised his stick. 'Stand ready. Stand light,' he instructed. He moved deftly to one side and then the other, his movements smooth as though gliding on ice. Robert matched him, a little unsteadily at first, but his steps became more fluid as he eased into the motion. *Just like Father taught me*, he remembered. *Balance on the balls of your feet, that way you will be ready for any sudden or unexpected movement.* He looked up to see his Father standing alongside Carrion, their movements synchronised, and Robert smiled. For a moment his eyes misted over and he wiped at them.

Carrion raised his staff, its end coming towards Robert at a more sedate pace to begin with, and he brought his stick up to meet it. 'Defend and attack,' instructed Carrion, his staff posing a threat to Robert who blocked the old man's attack. 'Parry my assault, block its passage and move beneath it. Lunge forward, repel my attack from above and attack from beneath. Let not a single strike reach your body, for it is soft and will yield fatally.'

Robert grew faster. He moved on the balls of his feet, the nimble technique his Father had taught him matching Carrion's teachings, and he found common ground between both men's methods. Each relied upon the need to strike fast and hard, yet to know when to retreat, He responded with ever-increasing vigour.

Carrion became more aggressive, his staff moving faster and with greater force, and Robert found himself caught time and again with its blunt end, but he sucked in lungfuls of air and steeled himself against the pain. His responses suggested understanding passed down from his father and grandfathers before him, each generation leading him towards this moment and whatever was to come, his abilities released from within.

Sweat coated his body as Carrion's teachings pushed him harder and faster, and then came a flurry of swipes and jabs that tested everything he had learnt. Carrion's strong uppercut was met with Robert's block and the boy rolled the old man's staff outwards and down before bringing his sword-stick overhead. His movement was fast, the threat real, and Carrion was forced to bring his staff upwards in a blinding motion to block.

A flash of metal caught Robert's eye, the bark-stripped branch he had trained and fought with transformed for a moment into a thin shaft of silver-grey metal that tapered to a fine point. The blade carried an ornate inscription along its length, its hilt and cross-guard polished and golden in the bright sun, and Robert's attack faltered as he stared at the sword gripped in his hand. Sweat stung his eyes and he sagged to his knees, mesmerized by the sight, but as he wiped at his eyes to clear them he saw the sword was once more a simple wooden stick.

Carrion lowered his staff and stepped back. 'I knew there was more strength hiding within you. Your father would be proud, as should you be.'

Robert breathed heavily. Words stuck in his throat as he struggled to deal with the vision he had just experienced. 'How was that possible?' he gasped. 'The sword, was it real?'

The old man leaned upon his staff, the exertion appearing to have sapped little of his energy. He looked uneasy at Robert's question but avoided answering, opting instead for instruction. 'You would do well to remember what you have learnt.' He indicated Robert's most recent lesson, but also something more, something Robert had not yet become aware of. 'While such skills may prove useful, some have a greater purpose than others. I believe your strength and character are more important than you know.'

A raven coasted above the trees, its wings wide as it circled once before settling in a flurry of dark feathers upon Carrion's shoulder. It put its beak to his ear and the old man leaned in as though listening.

'I will return,' Carrion said once the raven had finished. 'Archibald will watch over you in my absence.' He indicated the raven as it fluttered to the ground. The bird cocked its head as it peered up at Robert and strutted with an importance all of its own.

'But I need to go home,' said Robert, his fingers absentmindedly gripping the remains of the needle deep in his pocket. 'No one knows where I am. They'll think I'm dead or captured or something.' He climbed to his feet, the sword-stick discarded and forgotten. 'And where's Will? I need to see him. I need to tell someone where the Germans are hiding!'

Carrion held out a hand, the gesture intended to calm and reassure. 'All will be well,' he said. 'You must learn patience,' and with that, the hedgerow closed behind him and he was gone.

Chapter 14

Hidden amongst the bushes and behind the dry stone walls that bordered the village, the Home Guard felt exposed. They presented the front line of defence until reinforcements arrived, but that could take upwards of three hours at best.

Nobody knew when the attack would come, but the men understood they had little chance of stopping the German advance when it did. The most they could hope to achieve was to slow them a little if they were lucky, but twelve rifles and a handful of bullets against a division of battle-hardened German troops gave the men scant confidence.

Those without weapons had acquired pitchforks and other farm implements, but such tools were of little use against machine guns and grenades. The men were under no illusion that once the attack began they stood little chance of survival, yet doing something gave them the courage to stand their ground and go down fighting if they must.

It was one of the local men who was the first to notice movement, and the men steeled themselves for whatever was to come. A lone figure raced towards them, but whoever it was, it was no invading paratrooper.

The figure fell once but staggered to its feet, its legs white against dark shorts, its upper torso garbed in a grey jumper. It's Will Atkins!' claimed a voice, and George Semper was over the wall before anyone could hold him back.

'George! Wait! It could be a trap!' Stan Glover saw the danger that the farmer's hand did not. It came from having served with the King's Rifles during the First World War. He had seen such a trick used at the Battle of the Somme, the outcome as devastating as it was bloody.

George halted. 'But he's just a child!'

'Aye, lad, but it not be above 'em to rig one wi' a grenade. I've seen it before,' he added with a sour tone. His time in the trenches of the Great War had never left him and he had lost many good friends. He climbed over the wall and stood beside the other man. 'You go back. Leave lad wi' me.'

George knew the family well and felt pain as though the boy was his own, but he accepted the older man's experience.

'Stop there, lad!' Stan's voice was clear. Will fell to his knees and sobbed deeply.

'They got Robert!' Will cried, his words thick and barely audible.

'Who did?' Stan dreaded the answer but had to ask.

'Germans. They got Robert up by Carrion's Wood. He were behind me comin' down hill and then 'e weren't. They got him, I know so!' he cried.

Stan held his ground. He wanted to move forward but had to be sure before he did. 'Will, listen to me. I need the to hold arms out and turn around on spot.' When the boy didn't move he spoke again. 'Will, you 'ear me?'

The boy nodded, wiped his eyes and rose slowly. When Stan saw the boy was clean of anything he moved in and knelt before him. 'Now, don't worry lad. Young Robert's fine. Nowt so sure. Army's ont way and they'll soon send Jerry packing, you mark my words.'

And with that, Will collapsed into Stan's arms and he pulled the boy close.

*   *   *

Will's frame felt small and delicate in Betty's arms. Her youngest was still a child despite all he had been through, and she held him tightly. The worry she had felt over his safety now showed itself as an outpouring of love, and she held him as though she might burst.

Maude flung her arms around them both but Peggy held back, not wanting to interfere in their shared moment. Betty sensed the hesitation and opened her arms - what the girl must be feeling for the safety of her brother, Betty could only imagine, and as one they rocked and cried until they were exhausted.

When the hug parted there was an attempt to be happy, to talk about Robert as though he was in the next room, but they all knew it was forced. Nobody could bear to think he had been captured, or worse. The possibility was simply unmentionable.

Phillip had covered his emotions with bravado, his shock and worry turned into action, and he had gone to watch for the Army's arrival. He burst through from the kitchen what seemed like an age later, his voice full of excitement and hope. 'They're here!' he exclaimed. 'The Army, they're here! Trucks full of 'em! They've brought big guns an' all!'

Betty grabbed Will by the wrist as he jumped up from the sofa. 'Oh no, you're going nowhere, my lad. You're not leavin' this room. Now sit down and let Army find Robert. We'll hear all from 'ere, make no mistake, and I want you safe while Army do their job.'

'But I want to see soldiers,' he whined. 'They're looking for Robert and I want to see 'em. Not much can go wrong wi' village full of soldiers.' He looked to his brother. 'Phillip, tell Mother. Please.' He had a point.

Phillip nodded. 'He's right. Army's everywhere, three truckloads full. Wood's just over hill from 'ere so it likely safer int village than 'ere when fightin' starts.' He winked at Will, then turned his charm upon his mother. 'I'll look after Will. He'll come to no harm wi' me.'

Betty knew Phillip was right. He was a good lad, sensible in all the right ways and always had been. He'd risen to fill the gap left by his father and she couldn't be more proud of him. 'Go on then,' she said. 'But mind you do as you said, and you – ' she pointed at Will, 'mind you do as your brother tells. You've shown thesel' able to find trouble in empty 'ouse these days, and I can't take much more. Now scram!'

* * *

Professor Barnforth stood at the head of the clearing inside Carrion's Wood, Karl and Jakob alongside him. Both men had planned to disappear once their theft of the journal and the exchange of information with the Professor was complete, but that had now proven itself to be impossible.

All three men being seen together had created an unexpected complication. The illusion of a burglary from Professor Barnforth's study had originally been intended to highlight the professor's innocence, but the professor's decision to collaborate with the German High Command had been a dangerous game all along and had now taken a turn for the worst. Both the professor and the men sent to meet him were wanted men as a consequence, and until the invasion of Britain got underway in the coming weeks, they must resort to living off their wits if they hoped to evade capture.

Only the arrival of the German paratroopers offered any hope. Their parachutes had brought them to the ground between the coastline and the woodland's eastern border, where they had moved quickly into the greening gloom of Carrion's Wood. The shadows draped themselves around the men like a damp blanket, the gloom holding an atmosphere all of its own, but Captain Roland Schneider had little time for ill-founded worries. He had been handed a mission personally by Hitler and he was not prepared to let anything stand in his way.

Schneider was a brutal and unforgiving man. He held little tolerance for those beneath him and expected others to follow his lead to the letter. He also did not accept excuses. Now, as he stood overlooking the clearance, he sneered. 'You are sure this is the correct place? The Führer does not like to be disappointed and I would not envy your position if you were wrong.' A highly decorated officer with a reputation for being ruthless, failure under Schneider's command was not an option.

Not about to be ridiculed, Professor Barnforth retaliated. 'The military side of this operation may be your area of expertise, Captain Schneider, but the historical and archaeological decisions remain mine. Unless you are questioning my knowledge in an area you plainly know nothing about - and the trust, therefore, placed in me - I suggest you allow me to complete my work without hindrance.'

Schneider's face was a canvas of barely concealed outrage. He was not accustomed to being spoken to in such a manner and a response formed upon his lips, but Professor Barnforth beat him to it. 'And as we both know, the Führer has little patience for those who interfere with his plans. Pray such a failure does not fall upon you, Captain.'

'Well, I sincerely hope you are able to uphold your end of the bargain, Herr Barnforth,' said Schneider, determined to have the final word. He narrowed his mouth to a thin line of annoyance. 'And whatever historical trinkets the Führer tasked you to find had better be here.' He flicked his cigarette butt into the undergrowth and spat after it, the gesture a display of contempt at the professor's position.

The professor glowered at the other man's disrespect. He had spent years of his life following the most tentative of leads, from stone inscriptions weathered almost beyond understanding to barely distinct threads which promised so much but vanished like mist in the early morning sun, yet the story had failed to die. It was a legend that had tantalised the world for over a thousand years, and now its truth lay within his grasp.

He looked down upon a clearing between the trees, the space almost fourteen feet across, covered in dense undergrowth and dominated by a weathered stone at its heart. Trees had grown around its perimeter, their roots avoiding the space as though unable to grow there, but whether out of respect to what lay beneath, or some ancient fear, the Professor could not decide. All he knew was years of research had ultimately led him to this place, and it promised to be the discovery of a lifetime.

Turning his back on Schneider's disrespect, the professor surveyed the space before him and directed the men to clear the undergrowth. He wanted to see the woodland floor laid bare before him, its clues naked to the world for the first day in many lifetimes, but the men had barely begun when Schneider stepped forward with a gas cylinder strapped to his back. Men dashed from the clearing, two of them barely escaping before the flame thrower touched the undergrowth. The floor of the clearing burst into flames, the incinerated remains a smouldering heap of dust and ash as the searing heat choked the life from the woodland floor. Heat bloomed upwards in a rising cloud that spread through the trees. Leaves fell, singed and twisted.

'What are you *doing?*' cried the professor. He could not believe the brazenness of the man, nor his total lack of respect for such a historical site. Schneider pulled the trigger a second time and another burst of flame scorched the clearing.

The trees shivered menacingly within the gloom, but Schneider was unfazed. He played the flamethrower across their branches, an action that showed his disregard for anything other than his own arrogance.

Professor Barnforth was enraged. 'Get that thing away from here!' he shouted, his anger boiling over, but he was cut off as the shadows closed in around the group. The trees seemed to tremble in anger at the aggression, their branches moving like a crowd of skeletal limbs, enclosing the clearing in a wall of darkness, and in an instant, Schneider was gone.

It happened with such blinding speed that nobody had time to react. Schneider's cry filled the darkness, a fading shout of anguish and surprise that was cut short like the flicking of a switch, leaving an echo of silence. The heavy groan that followed was a statement of the woodland's anger and willingness to defend itself. There was no doubt about its intent.

The trees rustled, their branches moving as though in a show of strength, and the mangled remains of the flamethrower fell suddenly from overhead. It thudded into the clearing, the cylinder torn open in a gash of jagged metal, its barrel twisted back upon itself in a warning to those who had trespassed uninvited.

The men looked around anxiously, expecting another of their team to be whipped away at any moment, but the trees remained motionless, the air still once again. The situation was unlike anything the men had faced before and they had no idea how to fight an enemy they could not see, or the desire to try.

When the professor spoke his voice was quiet, his words carefully measured. 'Well, I think that indicates the need for care and respect. We are guests here and should do our best not to anger whatever is watching us.'

The men murmured agreement and the professor turned to the man alongside him. 'So, I believe you are now in charge, Oberleutnant Richter, but please,' and his words were directed towards everyone present, 'let us dig carefully. We have had quite enough shocks for one day.'

Chapter 15

Phillip and Will leant against a wall, mesmerised by the flurry of activity around the village green. Men stood in groups, rifles slung over shoulders as they listened to a briefing led by a Major and one supporting officer. It was an exercise in military preparation.

Major Simmonds' voice was drowned out by the growl of a motorcycle. It rumbled towards the assembled men before the rider killed the engine, allowing the motorcycle to coast to a standstill.

Eyeing the latecomer with disapproval, the Major continued the briefing. 'It is our responsibility to ensure no invading force gains a toe hold on British soil,' he continued boldly. 'Those who attempt such a deed will be met with the unresisting force of His Majesty's armed forces and the strength that gives this nation the name Great Britain. It is a name Hitler and the forces of the Third Reich would do well to pay close attention to, and a title worthy of the brave men who stand before me now on the brink of battle.' A ripple passed through the men, a sense of pride in themselves and a willingness to get the job done.

Simmonds picked up the pace once more, his words planned to bolster the men with energy. 'Your King and countrymen demand nothing less than our best,' he said, 'and our best is nothing less than we shall give to ensure the safety and security of these isles.' He paused momentarily, before adding, 'For His Majesty, The King!'

'His Majesty, The King!' shouted the men.

An officer stepped forward and the men drew to attention until the Major had stepped down. The command to dismiss was given, and as the men broke up to complete their preparations, a tall and willowy figure in green battle dress and webbing wove his way between them. His pouches were filled with equipment, the rank insignia on his shoulders marking him as a Captain, but an additional patch denoted a specialist unit, an insignia the Major had not seen before. The soldier snapped to attention and saluted.

'Captain Joseph Hammerton,' the officer said. 'SO44. Reporting as ordered.'

'Ordered? By whom?' asked the Major. He had not requested anybody additional to join his team and did not want any hangers-on. In his experience, such add-ons were often a hindrance and brought nothing of value. He sighed in exasperation. *Which busy-body has been interfering now?*

Hammerton took a sealed envelope from his pocket and offered it, the Major's name and rank inscribed across it in an elaborate handwritten script. 'From The Prime Minister,' he said. 'Winston Churchill.'

* * *

Robert had no idea how much time had passed. Time seemed to have no meaning within the seclusion of trees and bushes, but he knew he could not sit around and wait. He had to tell someone what he had discovered. He had to know whether his friend was safe.

'I'm going,' he said to Archibald. The bird flapped around his feet as though he understood every word. 'And don't you try and stop me!' It seemed the raven was attempting to warn Robert against such action, but Robert knew what he had to do. He pulled at the bushes, desperate to find a way out, and using the sword-stick he attempted to force his way through. He willed it to become a sword once again, but no amount of wishing produced a result and he cast the stick angrily aside. 'There has to be another way out,' he grumbled, but the bushes would not yield. He was trapped.

The crofter's hut filled the enclosure behind him. Its stone surface was rough and weathered, but cracks and crevices had formed between its ancient stonework to provide all manner of hand and toe holds. Robert hadn't had the opportunity to climb many trees back home in Middlesbrough, but since coming to live in the countryside he had become quite the expert.

Archibald flapped overhead, the air filled with the sound of his cawing as Robert scaled the front of the hut. He climbed over the lip of the building and onto the roof where a carpet of moss and grass had taken root. It was soft beneath his feet, his shoes making no sound, and he stopped to look around.

Was that a voice? A shout? He couldn't be sure. The wide-open spaces of the countryside allowed sounds to carry further, but the sound had been more urgent than regular conversation and seemed close.

He scanned the horizon from the farm buildings in the west to the coastal path away to his right, but there was no sign of the German paratroopers. No sign of Carrion. No movement or sound of any kind. It was eerily quiet, as though the sound of the world had been turned off.

Robert balanced on the edge of the rooftop. The grass below was long and tangled, an outcropping of buttercups and daisies scattered throughout, their colours like the smattering of an artist's palette. It appeared safe and he prepared himself for the drop before launching himself into thin air.

He hit the ground with a soft thud, his back to the rooftop. Everything around him remained silent until a rustle of grass told him he was not alone.

* * *

'Churchill?' Major Simmonds was concerned he had misheard. 'Winston Churchill?' His face registered disbelief, his mind a whirl at such a revelation.

'Yes, Sir.' Hammerton indicated the letter now in the Major's hand. 'My orders, Sir. From Downing Street. Number 10.'

Simmonds looked at the envelope as though expecting it to suddenly change or vanish before his eyes. He blew out a breath of disbelief. 'Stand at ease, Captain,' he said, before indicating the other officer present. 'This is Captain Weston.'

The men nodded to one another, Weston's mistrust of this unexpected visitor written across his face. 'SO44? I'm not familiar with your unit I'm afraid.'

'Not many are.' Hammerton tilted his head. 'To be frank, our work is quite secretive, hence why we answer to the Prime Minister directly.'

Weston nodded. 'That may be,' he said, his tone on the edge of being dismissive, 'but I am still the acting captain here and these are my men.'

'Absolutely,' said Hammerton. He held up his hands, palms facing Weston in a gesture that showed his wish not to tread on the other man's toes. 'And I can assure you I am not here to interfere or overrule any aspect of this operation,' he said. 'Consider my role a professional interest in the unusual.'

That made no sense to Weston. He was here to push back and capture a division of invading German paratroopers, with orders to kill if necessary. As far as he could see, Hammerton had no place in that. 'You do know why we are here?' he asked pointedly.

Hammerton stiffened. He sensed matters were about to become challenging. 'Yes, Captain, I *do* understand the implications of German boots on British soil.' His formality of tone showed his irritation at the other man's attitude. 'And my role means I understand far more about the reasons behind this German raid than you or Major Simmonds. It is why Churchill sent me here, and once your job is complete I can begin mine. In the meantime, I think it prudent we keep out of each other's way until such time as you have completed your side of the operation, don't you?'

*   *   *

141

The clearing had been dug out to a depth of four feet and soil was piled up around the edge like a mountain range. The work had proved hard and repetitive, the ground seeming to resist their efforts, but the men had worked in relays as others stood sentry duty along the wall that separated Carrion's Wood from the fields beyond.

Professor Barnforth inspected the stone that marked the centre of the site. Close inspection showed it to have six faces, each sloping gently inwards towards the crown. Each face had originally been inscribed with a pair of carvings side by side, but those that faced the northern side of the wood had all but vanished, obliterated by the weather and the ravages of time. Only the westward-facing emblems remained intact, and they were enough to cause the professor's blood to race.

He ran his fingers across the stone, his eyes widening, his mouth dry at the prospect of such a find. Could this possibly be it? Could this be the very stone for which archaeologists had been searching for so many years? For which he had been searching? The emblems matched perfectly with his years of research and he felt the pieces slip into place.

The professor's hands trembled with excitement, the excavation before him beginning to bear the first tentative fruits that went far beyond his wildest expectations. If only he still had the journal in his possession. If only he could check his findings! He shook his head in disbelief at the way events had unfolded, and not for the first time wished matters had been conducted differently. For the Nazis to snatch such an important find from his grasp, just as his research proved itself fruitful, was unbearable. He shook his head once again at the injustice of it all. How could it have all come to this? How could he have been led to this point so blindly?

A fresh layer of dirt had been broken and the men were busily removing it, each shovelful taking him closer to the prize, but it was not fast enough. He wanted to uncover the relics now, to place his hands upon the treasures that had lain beneath the earth for so long. His patience suddenly felt very thin.

'Oberleutnant Richter,' he called out. The man looked up from his digging. 'Your men need to double their efforts. They need to work faster.'

Richter was patient to a point, but his men were at full stretch. 'Professor,' he began, his tone abrupt and ready to chastise the professor when the shadows suddenly closed in. The ground beneath them trembled, the atmosphere heavy and ominous, and the broken earth rippled like water. The trees twisted and groaned, then all fell silent.

They had been warned.

*   *   *

The soldier put a hand to his bruised face where he had been shot with the catapult. He was bruised and bloodied, his eye almost shut, his cheekbone a swollen mass of flesh, not to mention the swelling in his throat. It hurt to swallow and he grimaced every time he did so.

Robert was pushed roughly in the back, the soldier far from gentle, but as long as he was forced to co-operate with the men he was determined to make the journey as difficult as possible. He glanced over his shoulder and taunted the soldier pushing him along. 'Nice black eye,' he said, mischief getting the better of him. 'What happened, you walk into something?'

The soldiers around him sniggered, their taunts good-natured, and although Robert had no idea what the men were saying he laughed along with them. It rankled the soldier – Gunter, if Robert heard correctly as the men ribbed him about his injuries – and he pushed Robert again. 'Rihig!' he hissed, which had to mean *Quiet!* or *Shut up!* or some such instruction, but Robert sniggered instead. The soldier dug him roughly in the back once more and Robert stumbled.

The wall to their left ended in an open gate overgrown with bushes. It offered some cover and the men crouched to listen as the sound of activity from the direction of the village caught their attention. The commander whispered orders and two men slipped over the wall and into the field beyond while the remaining men took up firing positions.

Silence filled the world, Robert's heartbeat and the whispered sigh of the wind through the long grass the only sound until a rattle of gunfire announced contact further down the hill. A wave of concern went through the men and they watched anxiously until they saw two familiar figures move quickly towards them. They returned fire as they worked their way across the field, each covering the other's retreat as they worked their way back to safety.

Gunter pushed Robert to the ground and held him there, his hand motioning for the boy to stay down. Robert nodded and Gunter slipped away to rejoin his men, their fire sporadic and more for effect than accuracy. Whether they could hit anything or anyone at such a distance was debatable, and with their attention focused elsewhere, Robert considered whether he should try to escape. He eased himself onto his knees and took a first tentative step away from his captors, but when a bullet whined over his head he screamed and dropped quickly to the ground. It seemed while staying with the group carried the danger of being shot at, running away brought an even greater likelihood of becoming a target. *Stay where you are*, he told himself. *Do you want to get shot?* He shuffled around in the grass and pushed himself as deep into the earth as it would allow. He could only hope it would be enough.

The men gave covering fire as the two paratroopers raced the final few feet and slid over the wall. Robert curled himself into a ball, his head pounding with the noise and tears of fright misted his e yes, although it was something he would never admit to.

As the group moved out Robert was hauled roughly to his feet, his collar bunched in Gunter's fist, and he was half dragged, half carried, his feet barely touching the ground before he found himself on the other side of the open gate and moving towards Carrion's Wood. It was the last place he wanted to go, but he had little choice in the matter.

The bulk of the tree cover lay upon the gentle slope that ran down to meet them, but the men still had open fields to cross before they entered its shadow. At their current speed they would be there in minutes, and as the gunfire behind them finally dwindled, Robert's attention became more focused on the tree line. At first he put it down to the wind, but quickly came to realise it was something more as the uppermost branches flicked and twitched, the shape of the forest changing before his eyes. He shuddered as he remembered how unnerving it had been the first time, but to go back in now, especially against his will, filled him with dread.

The soldiers picked up their pace as they moved into the final field. The ground before them had been churned and was uneven where enemy soldiers, the muzzles of their machine-gun poking from raised-up earthen embankments, lay dug-in across the hillside in readiness for the British assault.

A lump formed in Robert's throat as he was pushed the final hundred yards. His ears were attuned to every sound, his eyes everywhere as the woodland sprawled before him, its shadows ominous. His legs faltered at the prospect of stepping back inside and his pace slackened as a result. He dragged against Gunter's hand on his collar, a string of mournful *No! No! Nos!* escaping his lips, but Gunter thrust him onwards. 'Bleib in Bewegung!' he growled. *Keep moving!*

He sensed something bad was about to happen.

He was not wrong.

*   *   *

The Commandos left the village in three Platoons, Sword to flank Carrion's Wood and approach from the north while Dagger would attack from the south. Their objective was to crush the German paratroopers while Razor led a frontal assault from the west. The Germans would find themselves fighting three battles with nowhere to retreat, other than to the coastline which lay behind Carrion's Wood. At that point, they would have the choice to surrender or fight to the last man. It would take a brave individual to choose the latter option.

Will and Phillip stood by to watch as the men moved out, others joining them as the village emptied. A group of young women huddled by the roadside, their shout to the soldiers flirtatious, their blown kisses gladly received by the departing troops as they marched. They smiled and laughed in the shared joy of the moment and a land girl rushed forwards to throw her arms around the neck of one soldier. He lifted her off her feet as she kissed him and a huge cheer filled the air, such a light-hearted moment needed to lift the spirits of the men. Yet despite the good-natured antics lay an undercurrent of dread for the young men who marched out to battle, some of whom may not return. It was a strain that showed itself on the faces of villagers, many of whose sons had gone off to war. They wiped away tears and waved their handkerchiefs as much for their own boys as for those before them.

A chorus of shouts to *Give 'em a right pastin'* and *Show 'em who's boss!* was met with shaken fists and thumbs-ups, and then the crunch of boots faded, leaving the crowd with only smiles to paste over their fears and hopes to fill their hearts. They drifted away to sit and worry behind locked doors and shuttered windows, the safest place to be, yet Will's heart felt as though it had lodged in his throat and he could barely swallow. He coughed and took a ragged breath. Phillip put a hand on his brother's shoulder. 'You okay?' he asked.

Will sagged to the ground. He retched but did not vomit, his worry for Robert a weight in his stomach that would not ease. His friend was still out there, dead or alive he didn't know, but he hoped the soldiers found him before anything bad happened. He blamed himself for running and not looking back. If he had, they would both have been here watching the soldiers. Robert would have loved that!

'They'll find 'im,' said Phillip quietly. He crouched beside his brother and rocked him with an arm across his shoulders. 'They'll find Robert an' bring 'im back, you knows they will.' Phillip hoped he sounded convincing.

A man in uniform approached. He stopped before the boys, his face filled with concern. 'Are you unwell, son?'

Phillip stood up. He was well-known as being tall for his age, and his eyes were almost level with those of the soldier. 'Just upset, sir,' he said, his respect for his elders a natural way of speaking, and especially to a soldier; his father had taught him that as he joined up. 'His friend – ' He corrected himself, his voice a little softer when he spoke the second time. '*Our* friend be missing, sir. Bumped into German's on Monk's Hill, an' when Will turn 'round, lad weren't there. Not come back since either.'

The soldier nodded in understanding. 'Robert Cotterill. You're talking about Robert Cotterill.'

Phillip's expression questioned how the man knew Robert's name. 'Aye. He an evacuee; been stayin' wi us for last few weeks 'an become part o' family,' he finished, then asked, 'how did you know?'

The soldier nodded. 'The men have orders to find Robert and bring him back. By all accounts, he's quite the strong character.' He smiled. 'I feel confident he'll make himself known.'

Phillip grinned and Will climbed wearily to his feet. 'But what if Germans 'ave – ?'

The soldier reached out and grasped Will by the shoulder. 'Come now,' he said. 'You can't think like that. Where's your spirit? Your British determination? Robert will get through this, and so will we all. Faith is what is important now, faith in this country and its people, faith in the soldiers who will defend us to the last. Have no doubt, they will not let us down.'

There was something about the man that both boys liked. His manner was friendly, his smile warm and true. He felt approachable and genuinely concerned, a person they could ask for help should the need arise.

The man straightened himself up, 'Now,' he said, 'I wonder if you boys would be able to point me in the direction of Ravenscroft House. I need to make a visit.'

As the boys led the way uphill the soldier introduced himself as Captain Joseph Hammerton. He was easy to talk to and the boys were soon telling him about the events that led to the army's involvement.

Joseph was particularly interested in what they could tell him about Carrion's Wood and the old man who lived close by. 'With stories like that, there's usually a grain of truth lurking somewhere,' he said. 'It's just that time has a habit of twisting those facts, even though the truth is usually more straightforward than people think.' He looked over to Carrion's Wood as they walked, its shadows cool and distant, and the boys saw him peer intently as though searching for something.

Their route took them past the style Robert and Peggy had crossed to school that first morning before they headed up the final stretch towards the gate of Ravenscroft House. As they approached, Will slowed. 'You sure you want to do this?' he asked. 'Mrs Barnforth not be nicest of women. Folk round 'ere steer well clear and you be wise to do same if you wants my advice.'

Phillip punched his brother in the shoulder. 'Will, don't be so cheeky.' He looked towards Joseph and apologised on his brother's behalf. 'Will's not got much nice to say about Mrs Barnforth,' he said. 'Sorry.' He punched his brother in the shoulder again. 'An' he knows better than to talk out o' turn.' He fixed Will with a hard stare, but Joseph only laughed.

'You needn't go worrying, your opinion is safe with me. I've been forewarned about Mrs Barnforth, so I know to expect a difficult conversation.'

His boots crunched as he set off down the gravel driveway, his walk from the gate to the door seeming to take forever, but he turned and called back from the halfway point. 'Don't wait around for me. I may be a while.' He raised a hand. 'See you later, boys, and thank you.'

The boys remained against the gatepost, interested to see how Mrs Barnforth responded to an uninvited guest, but she opened the door before Joseph even had time to knock. Their exchange of words was brief before she moved aside to allow Joseph over the threshold. After a hard stare at the boys, the door closed with a heavy thud and the world reverted to silence.

Unsure what to do next, Philip and Will ambled back along the road towards the village. They quickened their pace when the crack of a gunshot rang out. It was hard to imagine that German troops dug in between the trees with British commandoes facing them down. Ravenscroft was too small and quiet a village for such things to happen, yet just over the fields battle was about to commence.

Another crackle of weapons fire sounded, the burst more intense, and Phillip grabbed at his younger brother's arm. 'Come on,' he said, 'it's startin'. We best get inside.'

*   *   *

Mrs Barnforth was a troubled woman. She had been visited by the local constabulary and the Home Guard, the accusation that her husband was a spy and therefore a traitor to his country something that shocked her. She spoke now to

149

Captain Hammerton in quiet tones, her usual abrasive manner somewhat subdued.

'No, Captain,' she said with dismay. 'I was unaware my husband had any involvement with Germany, and certainly not those who have invaded our village. I want them out, by the way, as soon as possible. This is our country and they have no right to be there. If they – '

The Captain raised a hand. 'Yes, yes, Mrs Barnforth, I agree, and your village will be returned to you, but there is much we need to discuss. Now, what can you tell me about your husband's research?'

The chair squeaked as Mrs Barnforth shifted upon it. She was visibly uncomfortable.

'Mrs Barnforth?' Captain Hammerton pressed the question again. 'Anything at all you can tell me, no matter how small, may very well be of importance. Please, consider carefully.'

The chair squeaked once again and she looked down at her hands, her fingers interlaced, her thumbs pressed hard against her index fingers leaving them white. 'I'm afraid to say,' Mrs Barnforth began, and then rephrased her answer, 'I'm *ashamed* to say, I know nothing of my husband's research.' She looked up. 'I have no interest in archaeology, and my husband has no interest in running the estate. That is the truth of the matter.'

Mrs Barnforth looked down at her hands again. She pulled her fingers apart and then wove them into a different pattern. Finally, she looked up. 'You see, Professor Barnforth and I have led separate lives for a number of years now, with only the girls holding us together.' There was regret in her voice and a touch of acceptance at things she could not change. 'He is a man driven by his research who lives in an increasingly different world to others, a world in which I am not included.'

She rubbed her thumbs against one another, her emotions threatening to surface. 'If the truth be known, my husband's trips away to London may have been hard on the girls, but they were a blessing for me.' She sounded increasingly deflated but continued. 'If he is indeed working for the Germans, then I knew nothing of it. You must believe me. Nothing whatsoever.'

'Has he had visitors?' asked the Captain.

She nodded. 'Occasionally. Official looking men, all very pleasant and respectful.' She considered for a moment. 'Impeccable manners, one of them. A foreigner, I believe.'

Now we're getting somewhere, thought the Captain. 'Can you remember his name? Anything about him? Even the smallest detail?'

Mrs Barnforth sat motionless for a moment, her lips pursed. 'He was an archaeologist, I believe, or at least that is what I was led to believe.' She sat quietly as she searched for a name. 'Strass, I believe he said his name was.' She nodded. 'Yes, that was it. Strass. A charming man. Quite charming.' Her eyes twinkled for a moment at the memory and she repressed a smile.

Captain Hammerton's blood ran cold. Strass was a name he knew only too well, and if he had any involvement with Professor Barnforth's research, then matters were of a serious nature. A great deal more serious, in fact.

'I think I need to look through the professor's study,' Captain Hammerton said, his pulse quickening at the implications of what he may discover. 'If you would kindly show me the way.'

The study occupied a room at the back of the house, its floor dominated by a large antique desk and chair. Paperwork sat in untidy piles, held down against disturbance by historical artefacts, books, and a fist-sized stone with a barely visible inscription.

A leather armchair and small table sat beside the desk, each littered with more of the same, while the shelves behind them held an extensive library. A collection of journals, notebooks, and string-tied papers sat amongst an extensive collection of books, all well-used and obviously of great personal value. The study held an air of devotion, as though belonging to someone whose mind was increasingly focused upon uncovering the truth of the past with little regard for the present.

Despite the disarray, Joseph saw the books and journals were arranged in two distinct groups with a space where one volume was missing. As he perused them he found that six held general archaeological findings, while the remaining twelve were specific to archaeological sites around the country – Lyonesse in Cornwall, St. Govan's Chapel in Pembrokeshire, and Alderley Edge in Cheshire to name but three. He opened further journals and found their contents held research on Glastonbury Tor, St. Michael's Mount, and Tintagel Castle. *But there must be something else here, something I'm missing.* He frowned with frustration. *Think, Joseph. Think!*

He looked again, their carefully written notes, their drawings meticulous in their precision and detail, and realised the research within each journal was focused upon a particular crest. *No, it's more than that.* He thumbed the edge of a page as he read, irritated with himself. *Come on, Joseph, think logically! A crest does not exist just for itself, it has meaning.*

He lay three journals before him, each open to a page showing a different crest. There was a link here, but what? He had never been one for giving up and perhaps there was something else, a clue hidden within a room of clues? It couldn't hurt to look.

Returning the book to its place on the bookshelf he removed all the leather-bound journals. Those that recorded general research he put to one side, the others he opened and lay upon the floor to study. Understanding eluded him. And why wouldn't' it? he thought. *You're no more an archaeologist than you are a historian. How can you possibly expect to unravel in two minutes the clues the professor has spent his life studying?*

Joseph's knees were stiff from remaining in one position for too long and he pulled the professor's chair towards him. He sat down and pinched the bridge of his nose between thumb and finger in an attempt to relieve the tension building there. His eyes felt tired and he closed them for a minute to think.

There has to be more to uncover, he realised, *a reason why the Germans have risked putting soldiers on British soil, and why the professor is involved.* And then there was Strass. His involvement proved a direct link between Hitler's belief in the power of historical artefacts and the professor's research. But what had he discovered?

Joseph sifted through the paperwork on the desk. Much of it held no immediate connection to the professor's research until he uncovered a sheet of drawings showing two crests paired together. They were aligned so their edges matched, both crests forming one image. It refocused Joseph's attention and he sifted the papers further to find wax rubbings of two different crests. The surface of the paper was pitted where the stonework had shown itself to be uneven, and as Joseph ran his hand over the paper he felt a thousand years of history pass beneath his fingertips.

If there were two pairings there would likely be others, Joseph realised, and he sifted quickly through the remaining piles. He found nothing, and returning to the journals he found another wax rubbing between the pages of one of the journals. He discovered a second and a third as he sifted, and Joseph hurriedly explored the remaining volumes. His eyes widened with each discovery and he gave a chortle of excitement like a child on Christmas morning.

He spread the rubbings before him, initially counting nine before adding the two from the professor's desk. If he was to pair them all that would leave one rubbing unmatched, and he realised there was something wrong. *You're going about it like a fool. Be logical, Joseph. Think!*

Joseph pushed all the rubbings to one side and placed the double rubbing before him as a start-point. He lay each of the single rubbings against its outer edges, discarding them when they did not match until he found his first pairing.

With three rubbings matched he began again, testing each edge until he found a fourth pairing and a fifth. They formed an arc as he worked, each pattern extending the curve until he found himself with something approaching a circle, except it wasn't a circle.

There was a piece missing.

Scraping the rubbings together, Joseph hurried into the hallway. He could only hope Mrs Barnforth had a telephone.

Chapter 16

Captain Reed was waiting with the journal when Joseph arrived. He ushered him through to the back room of the shop and closed the door.

'Thank you for this,' said Joseph, taking the journal. It felt good to have it in his hands. He was eager to delve into its pages but felt it only right he explain his findings first. Without the Captain of the Home Guard's professionalism, the situation could have easily turned out differently. Joseph held out his hand. 'We haven't been formally introduced,' he said. 'Captain Joseph Hammerton. Special Operations 44.'

Reed shook his hand, the shake warm and sincere. 'Captain John Reed. Home Guard. Not quite Special Operations, I'll grant you, but we do our bit.'

'Well, your contribution has certainly been noted. Thank you, John.'

'Glad to be able to help.' He indicated the journal. 'So, what can you tell me?'

Joseph pursed his lips. 'You understand what I am about to reveal will no doubt be deemed Classified Information, and must remain so. Are we in agreement?'

John nodded. 'Of course. It goes with the job.'

Joseph paused momentarily. 'Your knowledge of the professor's work and his involvement with the German forces only goes so far. It now seems the professor has discovered something of importance, something Hitler is willing to take great risks to obtain.'

'Well I would certainly agree with that assessment,' said John. After the events he had witnessed that afternoon, he was under no illusion that big plans were underway.

'It seems that in recent years Hitler has developed an interest in what some may term the mystical,' said Joseph. 'By that, I mean the supernatural, the spiritual, and while it isn't common knowledge, we are aware he has begun collecting those relics he deems powerful.'

John raised his eyebrows. 'Really? As if his plans for world domination were not enough, now he's dabbling in devil-worship.' He shook his head in disbelief.

'What we have here is not quite devil-worship, as you will see, but the professor's findings certainly fit under the banner of the unusual.' Joseph picked up his leather briefcase, snapped open its buckle and removed the pile of wax rubbings. 'Take a look at these,' he said. He arranged them upon the table, matching their edges as he had in the professor's study until only one gap remained.

John moved around the table as he studied them. 'Where did you find them?'

'Inside the professor's journals,' said Joseph. 'Each rubbing relates to an archaeological site around the country - Stonehenge, Glastonbury, St Michael's Mount,' said Joseph as he placed a hand upon three rubbings. 'Bamburgh. Tintagel,' he added, indicating two more. 'Each crest fits together seamlessly with those upon either side.'

John nodded. 'But there appears to be a piece missing.'

Joseph began leafing through the journal Reed had brought. 'Agreed. And if I am correct in my assumption, we will find it in here.'

The pages were crammed full of research in the same careful hand as the previous journals, the diagrams and maps again etched in meticulous detail. A map of woodland and the coast presented itself early on and John tapped a finger on it. 'We know where that is,' he said, and Joseph nodded, but continued thumbing through the pages without pause. There had to be a rubbing; every other journal had included one, so why not this?

He was about to concede defeat when he turned the final pages. Tucked between a pair of blank pages sat a tightly-folded sheet of tracing paper. The surface of the paper was waxy, the paper pressed flat, and Joseph teased it free and unfolded the paper with tentative fingers.

The image upon it was unlike the others, this rubbing little more than a decorative outline with no central crest. Nevertheless, Joseph held it reverently as though holding something of great age and fragility. He rotated it until its edges matched those of the two unconnected rubbings.

It fit perfectly, and both men studied the circle. Each rubbing was no longer a single entity, but now part of a complex pattern that formed a complete circle. It was quite beautiful.

'What is it?' asked John.

Joseph shook his head. 'To be frank, I'm not entirely sure, but circles have long been viewed as symbols of power and balance, of harmony and nature. The Ancient Greeks saw the circle as the first, simplest and most perfect form.' He shrugged. 'Who are we to argue?'

'I see their point,' said John, 'and whatever the Germans are doing up in Carrion's Wood, it must have something to do with this.' He tapped the circle of rubbings as Joseph flicked through the journal.

The paged flowed beneath his fingertips. 'There must be something more,' said Joseph. He scanned the pages with little idea of what he was looking for, hoping something would suddenly present itself, but even the idea seemed too good to be true.

'Go back to the map from earlier,' said John, and Joseph turned the pages until he found the map and lay the book open between them. A line from top to bottom indicated the coastline, with Whitby at the bottom of the page and Ravenscroft and Carrion's Wood above it. Brief notes were inscribed in three places, along with a drawing he did not recognize, and each of the symbols currently laid out on the table before them. There was no indication of any link other than their places in the circle, and even then it appeared as though some vital piece of information was missing.

'It does appear the professor was working towards something,' said Joseph. 'He has all the symbols but has failed to connect any meaning to them.' He pursed his lips into a line, his brow furrowed with frustration. 'What is it we're missing? What's the key?' He thumbed through more pages, stopping to read from a number of the professor's handwritten notes before moving on, then hesitated as he came across an eight-line verse. 'What's this?'

He pulled the journal towards himself and began reading:

> 'Raven had a heart so bold,
> Served his king on a throne of gold.
> Lived in a castle with a table round,
> Searched for a treasure never found.
> Where are you sleeping?
> What do you hold?
> What is your secret
> Never told?'

John tapped the top few lines. 'That's a playground rhyme. All the children around here skip to it. My daughters did. I've just not considered its meaning before.'

'So why is it in here?' asked Joseph 'And who is Raven?' He studied the text for further clues. 'There are writings by a knight named Sir Raven de Praye in the National History Museum.' He thought for a moment. 'His words are one of the only records that survive from the Dark Ages, but beyond that, I'm afraid I'm as lost as you are.'

John nodded at the significance. 'Sir Raven de Praye was a local knight who owned land around here. The village is supposedly named after him, but it's likely all just hearsay and legend. Nobody knows for sure.'

'But if it is the same knight, then this rhyme could be a link between legend and recorded history.' He re-read the words of the rhyme aloud, sounding each word carefully as he searched for further meaning:

'Served his king on a throne of gold.
Lived in a castle with a table round,
Searched for a treasure never found.'

He turned the page to reveal a continuation:

'Loved his King and brothers all.
Took his troth when duty called.
Walks the paths of the sword and shield.
Keeper of the truth, the Dragon's seal.
Ready to rise and defend once more,
This land of green from the eagle's claw.
Where are you sleeping?
What do you hold?
What is your secret
Never told?'

'Now that is a verse I have not heard before,' said John. He looked at Joseph and found him rereading the words, his lips moving as he digested their meaning. 'And Dragon's seal? Could that mean Uther Pendragon?' he finished. 'It seems improbable, but – '

Joseph proved to be a steadying influence. 'Now hold on, John, let's not get ahead of ourselves here. Many of the knights of old Modelled themselves on powerful creatures - Dragons, serpents and such like. While the thought that this could be something more is a delightful notion - and we both know where this *appears* to lead - the likelihood is this rhyme relates to the tale of a knight who simply gave his name to Ravenscroft.' His logic and calm centre were not what the other man wanted to hear. 'I'm sorry to dampen your spirits, John, but the road your thoughts are taking is a dead end.'

'But 'table round' and 'Dragons seal'? That's closer than simple coincidence, you have to admit.'

Joseph nodded. 'It is, but other tables exist around the country. There's one in Winchester that goes back to medieval times, plus plenty of sites where Uther Pendragon was rumoured to have held court. A round table is not a unique artefact, I'm afraid, and this is nothing but a simple playground rhyme. You said so yourself.'

John lay a hand upon the journal. 'But,' he said in a tone that indicated there was something more, 'that does not alter the fact that something up on the hill appears to support the professor's findings, something that should not be disturbed without careful archaeological excavation and recording.'

Joseph nodded. 'And if we are proved right, these emblems represent something of great interest.' He pushed the papers back inside the journal and the journal back into his briefcase. 'Whatever is being attempted up there must not be allowed to succeed, and I, for one, am not prepared to stand around and see such a site desecrated in the name of Hitler and Nazi Germany.'

Chapter 17

'Why have you brought the boy?' Richter was irritated. A prisoner – and a child at that - was the last thing he needed. With the impending attack from the British there was much to do, and the professor had not yet uncovered anything of worth. This mission was fast turning into a disaster.

'He knows too much.' Gunter was eager to defend his reasoning for bringing the boy with them. 'He poses a risk.'

Richter scowled. 'Bloody nuisance.' But what was he to do with the boy? He had neither the time nor the manpower to babysit him. 'Well,' he said, his English heavily accented, 'while you are here you can pay back for the trouble you have caused.' He handed Robert a shovel. 'Start digging.'

Gunter pushed Robert in the back and he fell forwards. The handle of the shovel dug into his side and he stifled the pain, but Gunter's laughter told him he hadn't been successful. He rubbed at his side and took a deep breath as he scowled up at the German.

'Something wrong?' Gunter smirked, his control over Robert arrogant, but the trees gave a restless shudder and for the first time Robert felt stronger within their shadow. It was a strange sensation, the fear and anxiety he had felt at being trapped within the wood replaced by a more comforting feeling, as though the trees had reacted to his pain. *Is that possible?* He rubbed at the ache in his side, its pain intense as he breathed, and the trees stirred as though at his discomfort. Where he had previously been frightened by their presence, something about their closeness was protective, and for the first time, Robert sensed the realistic possibility he would make it back home after all.

Something hit him in the chest and Robert took a step backwards, the stone coming to rest at his feet. 'Not so big now, eh?' said a voice, and Robert peered into the shadows. Karl stood before him, Jakob a few steps behind. Both men

161

grinned, but Karl looked battered and bruised, the gash on his nose particularly bad. His glasses sat awkwardly, their mangled frame misshapen. 'And do not think trouble-cause,' Karl added. 'Now, dig before I come make you.'

Robert bit his tongue. He ignored the pain in his side which had subsided to a dull ache, and the throbbing in his chest, and shoved his hands into his pockets. The needle his father had given him provided all the strength and belief he needed to know the Germans would never succeed, and he felt his cockiness return. 'Yes, Sir!' he retorted, and snapped to attention as he offered a salute.

A slap across the back of his head took him by surprise. It almost knocked him off his feet, but as he turned, fists gripped in retaliation and anger in his chest, a shout went up and the moment vanished.

'Professor! I have something!'

The Professor stepped down into the pit. 'Get back! All of you, get back!' He skirted the edge of the excavation, placing his feet carefully so as not to tread on anything of value.

The men did as instructed, leaving an exposed area where the professor knelt. The earth was rough where it had been broken, the large shovels having done all the heavy work they could. From now on it would need a more delicate approach.

Beneath a layer of loose soil lay oilcloth. It was intended to provide a waterproof layer but was old and cracked. There was every possibility whatever was wrapped within it had rotted after being buried for so long.

The professor brushed earth from the cloth, the ancient surface beneath his hands untouched for over a thousand years, but such contact between the ancient and the new caused the ground to tremble. The professor withdrew his hands, alarmed and unsure of how to proceed.

He looked around, the reaction to his touch filling the air with the grumble of a large beast. He looked into the shadows but saw nothing, and as the sound faded he reached out to the oilcloth once more. This time the light changed noticeably as the trees shifted position, their movements subtle, but enough to darken the atmosphere nevertheless.

Logic told him such a reaction should not be happening, but after what had happened to Captain Schneider, the woodland had proved itself to be anything but expected.

The professor raised his hands to show the woodland his good intentions, and then gently reached out. The woodland shivered, its tremor less threatening than the previous time, and the atmosphere settled into a sense of wariness. The professor sensed he had been allowed to continue, and feeling the edges of the oilcloth he gauged the object within it to be about two feet across and four feet long. It tapered away from him, its upper surface curved with the texture of nail heads and metal strips across its surface. He paused and then worked his fingers beneath its edges.

With a gentle pull he lifted the right-hand edge, and the shape lifted easily. The oilcloth was cracked and broken in places, groundwater and temperature changes having weathered the material beyond its expected use, and after so many years underground he was surprised it still existed at all. He lay the wrapped object beside him, treating it with the utmost care and respect.

The earth trembled beneath him, the air disturbed by distrust as the trees shuffled visibly, but the professor was too focused on the moment to notice. Nor was he aware of the snake-like roots that reached out for him as though prepared to snatch back what had remained hidden under their care for so many years.

Peeling back the edge of the oilcloth, the object was unmistakably a shield. Its construction and markings were unseen since the Dark Ages, but now they reflected the light of a different world. The professor shook with excitement, his hands trembling as he touched the object's surface, feeling its imperfections, its scoured surface and the gouges of battles long past. The shield had last been used by a knight to defend the honour of his King more than thirteen hundred years ago, and for it to be in the professor's possession now was dreamlike.

The trees made no effort to disguise their unease and Robert felt the tremor beneath his feet increase. His strength trickled away as he stood amongst the men, but they paid him no attention, their eyes focused instead upon the shifting darkness around them.

Professor Barnforth returned his attention to the impression in the earth left by the removal of the shield. He searched along it with his fingers, raking away the soil until he uncovered another piece of oilcloth. He turned to the men, indicating the surrounding area of earth. 'Clear this away. Use your hands,' he said firmly, 'but do not move anything. Leave it for me.'

The men looked at one another, the surrounding woodland of far more concern than the instructions of a self-important professor more interested in the dead than the living. After the fate that had befallen Captain Schneider the men were not inclined to do as asked, but Richter was their captain now and he was mindful of the need to succeed.

'The professor has given you an instruction,' he said, 'and I am not above shooting anyone who fails to comply.' He shifted the weapon in his hands to make his point. His superiors were not noted for their forgiveness and a failed mission was not something he wanted on his conscience. He waited a few seconds, and when no one had moved he thumbed the safety catch to the OFF position, the sound loud in the close confines of the wood.

Robert did not understand the German's words, but in any language his intent was clear. He swallowed the lump in his throat and stepped back until he felt the wall of the pit against his legs.

The men's eyes darted between trees and the muzzle of Richter's machine gun, and he raised his weapon a little higher to make his point. He pulled the trigger and a burst of gunfire stitched through the trees, releasing a curtain of leaves and twigs that fell to the ground as though in slow motion. It was the wrong thing to do.

Branches moved in on Richter like the limbs of angry men, brushing against one another as though sparring before a fight. Ancient timbers creaked and groaned, some splintering while others whipped about wildly after centuries of restraint, the true spirit of the trees let loose. Roots as thick as a man's body snaked visibly across the woodland floor, writhing and coiling like snakes as they reached for the offending man.

Behind Robert, the wall of the pit burst open and roots wrapped themselves around his lower legs. They thickened, their bonds coiling like rope, and Robert struggled to disentangle himself. Alarm filled his chest and his heart raced as panic choked him. 'Argh! Get off! Get off!' he cried, terrified at the sudden way he had been wrapped within them, and he clawed at the roots in an effort to disentangle himself. He fell forward, one leg free, the other wrapped in a coil that threatened not to release its grip, and somehow Robert found a rock in his hand, its edge broken like a rough blade.

With hacking motions, Robert sliced through the thinner roots, but others took their place. They were like the legs of an otherworldly spider, invasive and sinister, and panic rose again within his chest. When the stone fell from his hands he tore at the roots with his bare fingers, crying out in terror as he pulled helplessly against their increasing strength. 'Help me!' he cried, locking eyes with one of the paratroopers, his voice thick with tears. 'Please!'

Before the German could react, fresh roots sprung forwards and wrapped themselves around his other leg and his chest, and Robert felt them tighten. Others added their strength, and even as he tore at the roots, his hands cut and bleeding from pulling against their rough surface, fresh shoots split off, coiling upwards until his lower body was bound like a cocoon and he was unable to move.

One of the soldiers jumped forward and slashed at the roots with a knife, but despite the sharpness of the blade, his effort was futile. Robert's upper body was quickly encased in coils, his arms pinned to his sides, his body motionless, and he found himself helpless to do anything other than cry out in terror.

The soldier launched himself forward in a renewed attack, his blade hacking and slashing at the roots, but the effort was more for Robert's benefit with little hope of success. The soldier's chest hurt with the pain of seeing the child in distress - he had a son much the same age and could not bear to think of such an end for anyone, much less his own son. He snarled as his blade bit into the roots, and then another blade was cutting alongside his. Together the two men sliced and hacked, but their efforts were to no avail, and as the first man sobbed his apology the roots lifted Robert clear of the ground and pulled him into the shadows.

The soldier's anger exploded and he bared his teeth. In a snarl of rage, he sheathed his dagger and dragged his gun from across his shoulders, opening fire across the face of the wood in fury at the boy's demise. The machine gun hammered until the magazine ran dry, his finger clamped hard upon the trigger, the weapon's muzzle smoking. A hand was laid upon the top of the weapon and firmly pushed it downwards. 'It's over, Dieter. There was nothing more you could have done.'

Robert's scream echoed as he was hauled back into the shadows, his throat raw, his chest tight and hammering with fear at the expectation he was about to die. And then he was laid gently upon the ground, the sound of firing muffled, the branches above him moving erratically as bullets ripped through them. When the firing ceased the silence was like a blanket thrown over the world.

The roots that bound him relaxed and Robert sat up. He sobbed uncontrollably, his emotions battered, his head whirling until a hand fell gently upon his shoulder.

Carrion looked down upon him, a kindly smile on his face, and it was then that Robert realised the wood had not attacked him. It had protected him.

*   *   *

The men felt threatened, their safety after what they had just witnessed more important than Richter's instructions or the professor's demands, but the woodland continued to close in. The trees seemed to swell, their trunks and low-hanging boughs gorged as though they had grown to fill the space, their movement and noise terrifying, and one of the soldiers opened fire.

Branches whipped through the air where the paratrooper had stood, the air filled with his cry of pain as he was smashed to the ground. His body was instantly broken by the ferocity of the attack, and the other soldiers moved quickly, ducking and firing in response. Their gunfire was short and erratic, but their usual response to attack did little to push the trees back. Others paratroopers were knocked from their feet, weapons ripped from their hands and flung across the battlefield while roots stamped angrily upon them like the feet of giants decimating the battlefield. The woodland's rage was devastating.

A branch swung across his path and Richter ducked as he dodged the flying body of one of his men. He shouted to Karl and Jakob, but as Karl bent to grab a machine gun that had been thrown in his direction, a branch knocked him from his feet. He scrambled to regain his footing, panic fuelling his hurried scratching at the ground, but the branch grabbed him by the ankle and he was thrown high into the treetops. His screams stopped abruptly.

Hopeful of escape, Richter moved towards the back of the clearing. The trees moved to block his way and he sidestepped as Jakob was flung high overhead, but the space gained Richter a few feet and brought him closer to the professor.

His face white with terror, the professor chastised himself for his foolishness. Why had he not gone direct to someone in authority when the German demands had been put to him, when his family had been threatened? Now the situation had spiralled out of control and it was his own doing.

Richter lifted his weapon and fired a burst into an approaching branch, then dodged sideways as it snagged his jacket. He fought to free himself but the branch pulled at his clothes, his only option being to rip at his buttons and allow the jacket to be pulled from his shoulders. He dropped to the ground and grabbed for the shield.

The professor's throat was constricted with fear, his voice no more than a croak. 'No!' he shouted. 'That's a thousand-year-old relic! It's not to be – ' but Richter ignored him. He held the shield up and batted a branch away with it, the branch retreating to hover in the air like a cobra assessing the best moment to strike as another branch manoeuvered itself into position. Richter faced it down, spinning on his heel and moving into clear space, the shield holding the trees at bay. It was an unexpected advantage, and Richter pressed it to maintain his safety.

'You were right, professor,' grinned Richter. 'There *is* some ancient power here. I see now why the Führer desires such antiquities. He *will* be pleased!' He pointed at the professor. 'Dig up what you can while we still have the advantage!' he called. 'Time is short!'

'I fear that would not be wise,' said a voice.

The interruption took Richter by surprise and his head snapped around to see a figure within the trees, the old man's appearance disguised by the shadows. Richter pointed his weapon. 'Move into the light. Show yourself!'

Carrion's frame was wizened by age, his appearance dishevelled like that of a tramp. Age was apparent in every step, but the clarity of his eyes and his strength of voice told a different story. He spread his hands. 'I merely offer the benefit of wisdom.'

'I require no wisdom but my own,' Richter snarled. 'Now run along, old man, this does not concern you.' He waved the muzzle of his weapon as he made his point.

Carrion leaned upon his staff and stood his ground. He tilted his head, his demeanour that of someone who did as he pleased. 'I would advise you to reconsider,' he said. 'To do what you intend would be foolish.'

Richter glared, irritated by the slur. 'Foolish?' he said. 'I advise you not speak down to me, old man. *That* would be a foolish act indeed!' He turned quickly to fend off an advancing branch, the shield coming dangerously close to being struck, but the branch retreated at the last second and Richter stood his ground.

The old man shook his head at Richter's lack of respect. 'A true knight upholds the values of loyalty and truth, but your arrogance insults the honour of the knight whose shield you hold,' he said. His finger was raised in a wizard-like fashion, as though preparing to summon a spell. The comment drew Richter's anger, but Carrion had not finished. 'With age comes experience, yet it seems experience had taught you little.'

'My loyalty is to the Führer!' snapped Richter, the firmness of his tone illustrating how fanatical his devotion was.

'That may be so, but he who takes possession must do so for a reason. To simply covet is not enough. For more than a hundred generations such a truth has held true within this place, but I see you do not respect such values.'

'The Führer is the reason - the reason why the Third Reich is marching unstopped across all that lies before it. The reason why its enemies fall beneath its might, and the reason why he takes whatever he chooses.'

Carrion switched his staff to his other hand. 'Not all leaders rule by fear,' he said. 'Fairness and respect are held in higher admiration by those who look up to their leaders. It is a quality some would do well to learn. It is right and just.'

Richter's tone changed and he turned his weapon towards the old man. 'The Führer decides what is right and what is just. You would do well to remember that when the time comes for you to kneel before him and beg for your life.'

Chapter 18

Machine-gun posts had been set up on the three flanks facing outwards from Carrion's Wood. Stone from its walls had been rearranged to construct defensive barricades, behind which German heavy machine guns sat in readiness. The men were prepared for the British to put up a fight, but while the British had the disadvantage of fighting their way uphill, the Germans knew holding the wood against their advance would not be easy.

A sudden burst of gunfire from behind the outposts took the German sentries by surprise. Surely the British hadn't outmanoeuvred them to attack from the coast? The land there was thin and offered little cover, but in war anything was possible. Another burst of gunfire stuttered across the silence, its repetition telling a story all its own, and a ripple of concern passed through the men.

A hurried reorganisation sent half the men deep into the wood to support their comrades. They worked their way from tree to tree, their progress silent, their weapons ready should they encounter British troops, but with every step they encountered no one.

The atmosphere within the wood was uncanny, the trees seeming to bar their way and trip the men, leaving them no alternative but to draw their bayonets and cut the woodland back as they went. It slowed their progress and made more noise than they thought wise, but they had no option. The men grumbled between themselves, their words whispered, their exchanges filled with irritation and annoyance, but they pressed on deeper into the woodland.

A root wrapped itself around one of the paratroopers' ankles and he fell amongst the thorny vines of a bush. Its thorns scratched his face and neck and he cursed more loudly than he should as he struggled to free himself. 'I hate this place!' Bekker growled. 'If this is what Britain is going to be like, let them keep it, I say!' He cut away at the brambles and attempted to climb to his feet but a vine swung back to claw at his neck a second time. 'Argh!' he cursed. 'Get off me!' He slashed at the undergrowth in anger. 'Wretched place!'

Müller silenced him. 'Hush! You'll give us away!' He held out a hand and pulled the other man to his feet. 'Just watch where you're walking.'

Bekker grumbled but decided it was best to keep his irritation to himself. He spat on his fingers and rubbed at his neck in an attempt to soothe the sting, but the action only succeeded in aggravating the soreness. He hissed in discomfort.

Sporadic gunfire continued from deep within the shadows, the shouts and cries of battle growing louder as the men worked their way towards the site of the dig. They hoped to catch the British off-guard and help bring the battle to a swift conclusion, but the gunfire ceased suddenly and all fell silent.

Müller gave the sign to halt and the men held their position. They heard nothing, but after a few seconds, Richter's voice filtered through the trees. His tone was angry, his words unclear, but he sounded in control. Another voice responded, its quality older, the manner of his speaking unfamiliar, and the men crept forward until they entered the clearing.

The bodies of their fellow paratroopers lay strewn across the open ground, the roots of the immense trees coiling and snaking around them. The sight caused the men to fall into defensive positions, their eyes everywhere, their senses attuned to the sights and sounds of battle. Müller cleared his throat. 'Sir, we heard gunfire. We thought perhaps the Englanders had attacked from the east.'

Richter glanced towards Müller. 'I hope you left the perimeter well-defended, Lieutenant.' he stated, his tone curt. 'If the British attack now and you will have left us wide open - ' He did not need to complete his sentence, the implications all too clear. The thought of the British creeping up on them because of his men's incompetence was unforgivable. He waved the shield once more around the clearing and the trees drew back where they had approached him.

Carrion looked at the muzzle of Richter's machine gun. It was a less glamorous weapon than the finely crafted blade of a broadsword with its handle wrapped in leather, its hilt worked in the finest of metals to become the righteous weapon of a knight. Richter's machine gun was nothing by comparison; a blunt instrument with no glory attached to it and the man before him a poor replacement for the knights of his time.

'Many souls are tied to this place and they will permit nothing to leave,' he said, his manner matter-of-fact. He eyed the professor as he spoke. 'Your actions have angered those who rest here. You would do well to anger them no further.'

Richter raised his eyebrows. 'You think I am frightened by such threats?' He tapped the edge of the shield with the barrel of his weapon. 'You forget I hold all the cards, and it appears such possession guarantees safe passage.' He glanced around theatrically. 'I see no one to support you, while I am more than adequately reinforced. You would do well to go back to whatever hovel you call home while you are still able, unless you would like me to put a bullet through you here and now?'

Carrion sucked air in through his teeth. 'I think not,' he said calmly, his eyebrows raised in resignation. 'And I fear others may also take exception with your choice of action.'

'Others?' Richter sniggered. 'And who might *they* be?'

Carrion slowly extended a bony finger and pointed to where a knight stood behind the paratroopers, a white shift and cloak covering a chainmail vest that hung to his knees. An empty scabbard hung at his waist, the broadsword it had carried held point down upon the earth by large battle-scarred hands. The figure's presence was powerful, its size imposing, and the paratroopers shuffled nervously as the figure took a step forwards.

Professor Barnforth climbed to his feet, his hands held before him as he tried to appease the warrior. 'I'm sorry!' he cried. 'I'm sorry! I had no choice! I meant no disrespect. I – I - ' but his words were meaningless. The knight lifted his broadsword and moved towards the professor.

The paratroopers opened fire upon the knight but their efforts were futile. Richter just had time to bring his own weapon to bear before the broadsword pierced his chest.

He was dead before he hit the ground.

*   *   *

The sound of a firefight broke the silence. At first, the British troops thought the Germans had engaged one of the other units, the shouts and sounds of combat initially suggesting a short and fierce battle, but as they stepped forward they realised they were mistaken.

The soldiers halted two hundred yards out from the woodland. Whether its shadows hid anything unexpected they could not tell, and they moved forward in well-practised manoeuvres that gained them ground quickly. They regrouped against the perimeter wall before slipping over it, their weapons ready as they hit the ground.

Bodies littered the woodland where their enemy had fallen, the injuries inflicted upon them indicating the Germans had been attacked with a bladed weapon. It was obvious the paratroopers had not gone down without a fight, but the battle had been one-sided, the result as deadly as it had been brutal.

The evidence of battle was repeated all around the boundary wall, the aftermath equally gruesome. Whoever the Germans had fought, and from where their attackers had emerged, was unknown.

The men took up defensive positions and waited, the silence unnerving, and after a brief assessment the command was given to move deeper into the shadows. The men could only hope they did not befall the same fate as the Germans.

* * *

Joseph led the way uphill, the gap between himself and the captain of the Home Guard ever-widening. John had paused to get his breath twice - he was not as fit as he once had been or as fit as he believed himself to be, and the truth was showing.

Carrion's Wood was tantalisingly close, but Joseph slowed to let the men catch up. Private Salter, one of the younger men of the Home Guard and the only man fit enough to keep up, stood by his side. 'You knows Carrion's Wood be a strange place?' he commented in a veiled warning. 'What be so important tha' needs to rush to get there, if tha' don't mind me askin', Sir?'

Joseph considered his reply. He did not want to be rude to a man doing his bit voluntarily for King and country, but the man did not have the authority necessary for such information. 'Nothing I can tell you at the moment, Private,' he said. 'Not that I'm quite sure *what* we'll find, if I'm totally honest. I'm afraid there is a bit of a wait-and-see attached to this mission for all of us.'

Salter nodded. 'Right you are, Sir.' He knew enough to ask only what needed asking and no more.

'Good man.' Joseph shielded the sun from his eyes. It was a bright day and the full glare of the afternoon was upon them. It was too bright if Joseph was honest with himself, such strong sunlight washing out any details they might have seen. He squinted to bring the scene into focus but knew they would see little detail until they were closer.

The Home Guard caught up, their breathing ragged after the climb, their murmurs indicating how they felt about the place, but they were here for a reason and were prepared to follow through on their orders.

John mopped his brow as he stood beside Joseph and surveyed the scene. 'It's all very quiet,' he said, his voice low as if to prevent the wood from overhearing. 'There's normally movement or noise with the trees, even on a day as still as this.' He frowned. 'Restless, that's what the people around here say about it.' He pointed to the tallest tree. 'And that's the usual culprit,' he said. 'Bit of a traveller, that one. You can look at the treetops every day for a month and find him in a different place every time.'

Joseph nodded. 'So I've heard.' He continued his study of the tree line. 'Spirits have long been believed to inhabit trees as far back as biblical times, if you believe in that sort of thing.' He continued his study of the wood. 'The Celts and Romans believed in tree spirits, the Egyptians too; it's little wonder those beliefs still exist today if you consider how much emphasis our festivals place upon the produce of the natural world for harvest time, Christmas and the like.'

John grunted in agreement. 'Well, if you watch Carrion's Wood long enough you'll see all manner of strange things to support those beliefs.' He gave a tilt of the head in recognition of what was to come. 'And I think you will find Carrion's Wood unlike any place you have visited before.'

Joseph pursed his lips. *If you'd seen some of the things I've seen, you'd know what strange was*, he contemplated, but instead added: 'That said, we must be cautious.'

Chapter 19

Robert moved out of the shadows, the trees agitated at his movement, their branches flowing as though in a slight breeze. The woodland had taken on a sense of growing calm but Robert sensed it could just as easily be stirred back to action should a wrong move be made. He eyed the scene before him where German soldiers littered the floor of the pit as though sleeping. He knew that was not the case.

Carrion turned him away. 'This is not something for young eyes to witness,' he said. 'You should have remained within the trees. They are sworn to protect you.' He hoped to spare the boy any further distress and walked Robert back towards the tree line. The edge of the pit hid the scene below, but a tall figure dressed in white caught his attention and Robert stepped around the old man to look.

The figure moved slowly across the base of the pit, his appearance grained as though with great age. Robert instinctively knew the figure was out of place, as though from another time, and he watched, mesmerised, as the knight knelt by the body of a fallen German trooper.

'Who's that? What's he doing?' Robert took another step forward and Carrion sighed, resigned to the fact the boy had seen more than was right for one of his age.

'He honours the dead, paying respects to the deceased as though one of his own.'

'Why? The Germans are the enemy.'

'Even on the battlefield, the fallen should be honoured,' said Carrion. 'Such an act is only right.'

Robert watched as the knight laid a hand upon the body of the soldier. The earth around the fallen man churned and parted, and the body slid beneath it. 'Who is he?' asked Robert again, fascinated at a sight many would find morbid or upsetting, but after listening to Carrion's words he saw the man's actions as caring and respectful.

Carrion placed a hand upon the boy's shoulder and knelt, his voice barely a whisper. 'He is one of the twelve.'

Robert looked up. 'You mean there are others?'

Carrion nodded.

'Where did he come from?'

Carrion indicated with his finger. 'He has always been here. The wood, the trees, they are his resting place.'

'You mean he's dead?' Robert's voice was louder than he had intended it.

The old man grasped his staff, the action slow and reserved, much as the knight had grasped the hilt of his sword. He paused before speaking. 'Not dead,' he said at last. 'Waiting. All warriors deserve the respect of their victor, but few have shown themselves to uphold such beliefs in recent times.' He paused and they watched together as the knight moved on, kneeling by another of the fallen paratroopers. 'Honour is one of the five codes a knight must live by. It defines the man and is the manner by which he conducts himself. Without it, he is not worthy of the title of Knight.'

A flap of dark wings disturbed the moment and Archibald perched upon Carrion's shoulder. He nodded as though listening, then turned towards Robert. 'It appears visitors will soon be with us,' he said, indicating the western side of the wood.

The shadows remained dark, but the tree line became agitated as figures moved through it. Carrion climbed to his feet as they approached and he stepped forward. Weapons were immediately trained upon him. 'Halt! Do not move!' came the command. 'Show your hands!'

Carrion grasped his staff rather than doing as instructed, and a group of men broke off from the seclusion of the trees to fan out around him. Others dropped into the pit where the knight, still bowed upon one knee, turned his head at their presence. The coldness in his face was more than a match for their courage, and when the men did not retreat, his grip tightened upon the hilt of his broadsword.

'Unless your men wish to meet a similar fate as those already fallen, I would advise them to withdraw,' Carrion said matter-of-factly. 'Sir Lamorak only wishes to pay his respects to the fallen. Allow him that dignity, if you will.'

The soldiers stood their ground, the air thick with possible outcomes, but a fresh voice called out across the clearing. "Respect may be earned in battle, but should also be offered to the defeated, for we are all men.' Are those not your words, Sir Raven de Praye?'

Carrion searched the shadows for the origin of the voice. He had not been called by his full name and title for over a thousand years, neither had he expected his own words would be remembered, but someone had recounted them exactly.

As he peered into the gloom, a tall man stepped forward. He carried an air of strength and decency, but another soldier intervened. 'You have no authority here, Captain!' Major Simmonds did not appreciate the unexpected intrusion, but Joseph cut him off. It was not something he would normally do, but in this instance, his authority was of the highest level.

'I think you will find Churchill's authority is authority enough,' he said flatly. He fixed the Major with a determined stare. 'For their own sake, tell your men to stand down,' he said. 'Immediately.'

Simmonds was more than prepared to fight his corner, but disobeying orders from Downing Street was a surefire way to find himself severely reprimanded, demoted, or both, and his career was worth far more than that. He bit down on a sharp retort and turned instead to Captain Weston. 'Take your men and secure the remainder of the wood. Be sure to account for every member of the invasion force.' He indicated the knight in the pit below. 'But exercise caution; we do not wish to lose any men. Is that clear?'

Tension remained balanced on the pull of a trigger as the men moved out of the pit, but Joseph ignored it. He had matters of great historical significance to deal with and made his way carefully around the rim of the pit. 'You *are* Sir Raven de Praye?' he asked, anticipation barely concealed within his voice as he stood before the old man.

Carrion tipped his head. 'I am, good sir.'

Joseph looked down at the boy beside the old man. 'And you, I assume, are Robert?' The boy gave a weak smile and Joseph wagged a playful finger. 'I have heard a great deal about you today, son. It appears you are quite the man of the moment,' Robert's smile widened and Joseph continued. 'You have a number of people eager to see you.'

Sir Raven put an arm around Robert's shoulders. 'Some people have more about them than they know, and this young man has most certainly shown the honour and valour expected of a knight. He is one to watch.' He patted Robert's shoulder and the boy grinned up at him. After their initial meeting he had come to like and trust the old man. He sensed their friendship was far from over.

'And you, sir, what is your title?' Carrion asked of Joseph. He sensed this man was not someone of concern but rather an ally. He spoke with respect and dignity, something missing from the soldiers he had encountered in recent days.

Joseph straightened his shoulders. 'Captain Joseph Hammerton,' he said. 'I am here on the instructions of His Majesty's Government to ensure the safety of this site and the treasures contained within it. You have my word, Sir Raven, that nothing will be removed from this place. Its protection is of great importance and had we known of its existence earlier, procedures would have been put in place to protect it.'

The old man sighed. 'I sense the goodness of your intentions, all of you,' he said, looking around. His voice was sincere, yet tinged with sadness. 'If only others had been as respectful, matters may have ended differently.' He indicated the remains of the site before them. It was stripped of its natural cover and had been dug over by those who wished to possess what was not theirs to take. 'It has been my duty to guard this place and those who rest within it until such time as they are needed to defend this great land once again.'

Carrion's words caught Joseph off-guard. 'And is this the time? Are the knights about to rise? Goodness knows we need them now more than ever.' Even as they spoke, Hitler's forces were massed across the channel, the Luftwaffe probing the country's defences from overhead. He shook his head in dismay. 'If there was ever a time we were in need, this is it. Their aid would not go unheeded.'

The old man shook his head. 'You require not their aid, for victory favours those with goodness in their hearts. Ultimately the enemy of freedom will be defeated, yet sadly, greed has caused such an avoidable waste of life.' He peered down at the remaining bodies, most of who had been claimed by the earth.

Joseph's response was more of a statement than a question. 'So the knights rest here, in the wood?'

Carrion indicated the breadth of woodland. 'This has long been their resting place. The trees, the earth, the very soul of the land holds their spirit.'

Joseph's face creased with a smile of realisation. He was starting to think John had been right.

'And what of the round table?' he asked, his chest tight with tension at the possibility. 'Does it lie here also?'

Carrion leaned upon his staff as he considered the question. To answer truthfully upheld his vow of honesty, but doing so broke his vow of loyalty and risked the security of the round-table, which he had striven to protect across the centuries. Conflict burned within him, its pain deep, its angst wrapped around his heart like a coiled serpent. What was he to do?

A voice from long ago filled his head, the voice of his King and brother in arms: *Trust in others must be accepted as well as offered, only then will goodness and truth outweigh the evil and deceit of man. That we must remember, else the world risks descent towards a far darker place than it deserves to be.*

Those words had been upheld by the Fellowship of Knights, the table around which they had sat uniting the land

181

and its people under the strong leadership of one man. One King.

'Come,' he said, turning towards Joseph and Robert, his decision made. 'The time has come for the truth to be heard once more.' And with that, Sir Raven de Praye, Guardian of the Twelve, Protector of the Round, stepped down into the pit.

Sir Raven nudged the German machine guns aside with his staff as though disgusted by their presence. Robert kept pace beside him, the old man's presence offering security and comfort amongst such uncertainty.

Three shields lay upon the earth, two side by side and covered by oilcloth, the third a few feet away, its protective layer peeled back across half its surface. It was dulled by age, a thin coat of mould dusting its metallic surface where it caught the light. A raised emblem was visible beneath the covering. Sir Raven bent to retrieve it but stopped as Robert broke the silence.

'Why didn't you tell me your name?' Robert asked. 'Your proper name?'

Sir Raven looked down on the boy, his face lined by tiredness. 'A name is often a reflection of the person we are or the person we have been,' he said, his expression honest and truthful. 'Is Carrion not a fitting name for one who counts the birds as his eyes and ears?'

Archibald fluttered his wings as though adding agreement to Sir Raven's argument, but the boy took little notice. 'With no one to speak my true name, I would be surprised if it were remembered a thousand years hence,' he said quietly. He tickled Archibald upon the breast with a long finger before continuing. 'As long as one is remembered in some way by their actions, then their story is not forgotten, even if their name is.'

'You are not forgotten, Sir,' said Joseph. 'Nor will you be. Your deeds have written their own history, your story recorded in manuscripts held in safety even today.' Joseph pulled the journal from his pocket and opened it to a page, marked not by him but by the professor. He scanned it briefly before reading aloud.

'And so I, Sir Raven du Praye, eldest son of Geraint du Praye and Monique du Praye, advisor and knight to the lawful and righteous King of Britain, do take on the duty of Guardianship of the Twelve, Protector of the Round, and Watcher of the World, until a time when the knights are to be called upon to rise once more.'

Sir Raven sagged under the weight of his own words, spoken so long ago in the presence of his king and the knights of the round table. 'I remember those words,' he said, his voice hushed, emotion underlying the moment, 'but I did not expect to be called upon to fulfil my duty so swiftly.'

'Yet fulfil it you have,' said Joseph. 'Your duty is done, Sir Raven. Your king would be proud.'

Sir Raven lay his staff upon the ground and touched the oilcloth covering a shield, his fingertips lingering upon its surface after so long. 'Yet I failed,' he said sadly. 'I allowed the hands of evil to disturb that which I was tasked to protect.' He shook his head as he ran a hand across the oilcloth, his voice little more than a whisper. 'Forgive me, my king.' A teardrop blossomed upon the surface of the oilcloth, a second alongside it, and Sir Raven sank to his knees. 'Forgive me.'

Archibald's cawed once, his cry of distress mournful in the silence. Even the trees remained motionless.

'Guardianship and respect run hand-in-hand,' said Joseph, 'and you have shown both with undying loyalty. No man here could say you have failed.'

Sir Raven nodded as though in acceptance, then lifted the shield before him and placed it within an indentation in the earth. It fit perfectly, the outer layer of oilskin folding into the hard-packed earth like a finely-cut stone within the setting of a ring. Sir Raven crouched before it, his hand upon the oilskin, his final touch accompanied by a silent renewal of his vow to protect the wood and all it contained. He lay the second shield alongside the first, their edges touching, and he smoothed loose earth over their surfaces. Despite all the disruption to the woodland site, doing so remained his duty.

A tremor ran through the ground, the disturbance more of a sensation than physical, as though the woodland had reacted to Sir Raven's touch. A trickle of earth fell from the edge of the pit, its fine grains moving like the gentle wash of an incoming tide to cover the shields until no trace of their existence remained.

By rights, Sir Raven should have replaced the final shield, completing the circle to which he was watcher and guardian, but Robert, a boy quite unremarkable in most cases, but whose fate was unknowingly tied to Sir Raven du Praye and the secrets of the ancient woodland, stepped forwards and picked up the shield before Carrion could rise.

The shield trembled beneath his fingers, the sensation startling, and he looked to Carrion in surprise. He hoped the old knight would advise him or offer a few words of reassurance, but instead Carrion climbed to his feet and rested against his staff. When he nodded, Robert realised the old man had offered his permission to continue, and so he stepped forwards, sensing the importance of the task, and returned the shield to its resting place.

A fine layer of dirt slid across the protective oilskin until only the shield's outline remained, but that too soon vanished as the shield slid beneath the earth, reclaimed once more by the woodland to the place where it had lain undisturbed for more than a thousand years.

Chapter 20

Silence fell across Carrion's Wood. It was as though the world stopped turning, the woodland becoming a place of sacred importance against the world outside.

A layer of mist, thin like autumn's first chill, hung around the base of the trees. It flowed into the pit where it thickened, the true depth of the pit lost beneath it, and the soldiers renewed their defensive positions. Against what, they did not know.

'Your men will not be in need of weapons,' called Sir Raven. The atmosphere deadened the tone of his voice, causing it to sound flat, but his warning was well-meant.

'Such a warning is for their safety, Major,' Joseph added. 'Do you wish to be responsible for their deaths if one of them should misfire?'

Simmonds considered the situation, unhappy about taking the advice of a man he outranked, but ordered the men to stand down nevertheless. It was a decision he would not come to regret.

The mist thickened to a rising fog and lights appeared within it, one to the right of Sir Raven, one opposite, then two to the left. More appeared, waist-high within the pit, each light widening to take on the form of the shield buried in the earth beneath it. Where the edges of the shields touched they became one, the linear patterns Joseph had first discovered in Professor Barnforth's study emblazoned across their surfaces like glowing script.

'Oh, my!' Joseph grabbed the journal and pulled free the rubbings. He shuffled them, matching each to the shields which glowed before him, his eyes wide with disbelief as he saw the professor's years of research proved correct. What a shame his motives were so misguided he was not able to see the result of his labours.

185

Joseph looked to the rim of the pit. 'John! Get down here!' he called. 'You need to see this - the shields, the symbols - ' his voice held a whisper of dismay, 'they're all here!' He did not have the words to express his emotions in the raw passion of the moment and he breathed deeply to calm the pounding in his chest. He had seen many unusual and unexpected things in his role with SO44, but something about this particular moment choked him like no other.

Sir Raven stepped back as Sir Lamorak took up position behind one of the shields. The knight rested his hands upon the hilt of his sword and bowed his head once more in respect as other figures appeared alongside him. Their outlines were thin at first before taking on a more solid form, each knight bearded, their robes similar to that of Sir Lamorak, yet each was subtly different.

'The table,' said Joseph as John stepped up beside him. 'The shields are the table. Why didn't we see it before?' He read from the sheet, pointing out each knight and shield in a clockwise direction: 'Sir Lancelot; Sir Gawain; Sir Geraint.' He continued around the circle – around the table – until all the names and shields had been accounted for, except one. A blank shield stared at them like a toothless gap, stark in contrast to those which surrounded it.

'Who are we missing?' Joseph flicked hurriedly through the journal, his fingers nervous upon the pages. The possibility of finding a missing link at such a late stage was all but impossible; after all, he had found no twelfth name, no evidence in all of the rubbings and papers back in the professor's study, so how could he expect to uncover it now?

And then he realised the truth, and the wind was forced from his chest as though he had been punched.

Chapter 21

Robert felt uneasy as the mist swirled around his legs, but found its touch calming rather than the chilling sensation he had first expected. He watched as Sir Lamorak moved towards a position on his right, the knight's tread across the earthen pit slow and silent - *ghost-like*, he thought - yet somehow the figure was anything but ghostly. The knight's presence spoke of life, his threat to anyone who challenged him a power that proved his existence, and something the German paratroopers had learnt to their own cost when they opened fire. It was a lesson the troops who watched now from the rim of the pit would do well to heed.

The movement and spirit of the wood suddenly made sense. Robert realised the worry he had first felt on entering was no more than a childhood fear of the unknown, a fear any child might conjure from night-time shadows beneath the bed or strange sounds in the night. No, the woodland shadows had not been stalking him, rather they had followed, their intentions watchful and protective. *No harm will befall you,* Carrion had told him, and now, as a sense of belonging overwhelmed him, he understood.

The shield between Sir Lamorak and Sir Lancelot beckoned as though Robert was being welcomed home, and swept along by emotion, he stood behind it.

The shield before him was blank at first, its surface as unmarked as the day it had been created, but as he watched an elaborate tracery of light etched itself across its face. The pattern was complex, its detail spreading from shield to shield, highlighting each emblem and embellishing it with a latticework so detailed it appeared fragile. The shields shimmered within the mist, their glow spectral, their appearance regal.

The knights remained motionless, the silence within the pit total until as one, they descended to one knee and bowed their heads before him in a sign of fellowship and allegiance. From somewhere high above a halo of the purest light illuminated Robert's head. It cast his hair within a golden crown, and as the knights offered up their swords and pledged their lives to his service, it danced from their polished blades as though from a mirror on a summer's day.

The swords formed a circle around the boy and each blade resonated in harmony with its brothers. The chime of metal rung clear upon the still air as though a bell had been struck, and as Robert looked out over the knights and their shields, he realised he was standing where history intended him to be.

Chapter 22
One year later

Peggy and Robert soon learnt that rural life was far more exciting than anything they had expected. Helping around the farm often left them smelly and dirty, but the fresh country air and close contact with animals made up for any initial distaste. They could not have been happier.

Betty had gone out of her way to make them feel as welcome as possible, and after their difficult start in the village, they quickly felt guided by their new family in ways they could never have imagined. They helped to plough the fields for planting in the spring and harvested the crops in the autumn, they ate fruit and vegetables pulled fresh from the ground in the summer and collected silage to feed the cattle through the winter. They found the summer hot with sun-bleached days and endless blue skies, the winter bitterly cold with snowdrifts that buried cattle and wiped away the landscape, leaving the village cut off for days on end. Throughout it all, they had come to view the natural world as it really was, and it fascinated and strengthened their spirit in so many ways.

Mother came to visit several times throughout the year, the change in her children startling, but it was a change that warmed her heart with the love shown towards them by others. *My children arrived frightened and mistrustful, their mistreatment casting a cloud over their young lives,* she had told Betty during one of her visits. *Yet here they are, happy, trusting and fulfilled. I could never have imagined such a thing.* She paused to wipe a tear from her eye before adding: *Their father would be so proud.*

And with that, she took Betty by the elbows. *Thank you,* she said quietly. *Truly, thank you.*

Chapter 23

After almost six years of bitter fighting, Nazi forces had been forced back from Europe and into the heart of Germany. Surrounded by Britain and its Allies, Hitler retreated to his underground bunker and took his own life. German forces surrendered over the following three days, and on the 8th May, 1945, the war in Europe ended.

Ravenscroft, like every other village and town across the country, celebrated the return to peace. Tables lay end to end along the High Street, loaded with celebratory sandwiches and cakes, buns and fancies baked from the meagre supplies of a war-ravaged village, while bunting and paper decorations hung from street lamps and windows.

Children raced around the village green, their game of Tag widening as others joined in. The release of tension as the war came to a close eased, and as the morning of VE Day unfolded, the village prepared to celebrate its freedom with a street party that would never be forgotten.

Barbara Cotterill had made the journey especially, invited by her children and the Atkins family to celebrate along with them. She watched, proud of the young woman her daughter had become, her hair neatly styled, the first blush of womanhood evident across her features as Phillip led her away by the hand. She smiled. Phillip seemed like a nice boy, and from what she had seen, he treated her with respect. It was everything she could ask for.

Robert, by contrast, had grown tall, his features maturing to echo those of the man she had loved. His eyes carried the same deep blue as his father, but also a glint of mischief. Light danced in his eyes like the flying embers of a summer bonfire, and although a rebel burned within her boy, Barbara knew he would be a leader who would always do the right thing. He was a boy with his father's heart, after all.

The call to eat went out and bodies filled a mismatch of chairs and stools. Eager hands filled empty stomachs as laughter filled the air, and as the table cleared, adults raised their glasses to absent friends.

Robert and Will sauntered away, leaving the noise and festivities for the younger children. They followed the hedgerow that bordered the fields below Carrion's Wood, its trees no longer a threat these days, and he often found himself staring wistfully towards the shade upon the hill.

He often dreamt he was back inside the wood, Sir Carrion leading him along its shaded pathways as the wood opened its heart to him. It was as though the old man had a secret to share, as though he was trying to show Robert something, but he always awoke before the old man was finished, his final words lost in the haziness of rousing. The wood was deemed out of bounds now, entry to it forbidden by order of the Ministry of Defence, but perhaps he should take a walk up there again anyway. Perhaps he would see Carrion. Somehow, it felt like the right thing to do.

'How much longer is tha' stayin'?' asked Will.

The words broke Robert's train of thought and he turned with a frown. 'Mmm?'

'How much longer is tha' goin' to stay?' repeated Will. For some of the evacuees, arrangements were already made for their return home, but there had been no mention of it for Robert and Peggy. Will secretly hoped they would stay. He and Robert had become firm friends, and Maude was already upset at the thought she might lose Peggy. Phillip too, but for different reasons.

Robert shrugged. 'Dunno. Mother hasn't said much, other than our street was bombed the other week and looks like it might have to be knocked down. She's been living with Mr and Mrs Bell in the next street, but they've taken the Robinson baby in as well after his parents were killed. Pulled him from the rubble, Mother said, so it doesn't look like there's room for us.' He shrugged again. 'She's trying to sort out somewhere new to live but said everyone's in the same boat.'

Will nodded. 'What about your Father? You 'ad any more news?' Bernard Cotterill had been missing in action for the past six months with no word and an ever-decreasing chance of him finding his way home. It had put a dampener on all their spirits, casting a cloud over their mood and pulling them up sharp with every knock at the door.

Robert's face fell, the possibility their Father might not come home increasing with every day. He frowned and turned away, not wanting Will to see the emotions play across his face. He shoved his hands into his pockets and kicked at a clump of grass before turning back towards his friend.

'Can't the stay 'ere?' Will was grasping at straws, desperate to find a solution. 'We can make more room, move things 'round. I'll talk to Mother.' He stopped walking, worry on his face. He *had* to find a way!

'Mother does like it here,' Robert added. They all did. Ravenscroft offered warmth and a welcome that wrapped itself around them like a favourite blanket. Both he and Peggy had made good friends - *family* if he was honest – and neither of them felt the desire to leave.

A shout caught his attention, his name being called out upon the still afternoon air, and he looked up. 'Robert! Robert! Come quick!' Figures were running along the road towards him, Peggy and Phillip, Maude close behind, their eyes filled with tears.

Robert's brow creased and he was instantly worried. He started running, his long legs and extra few inches in height giving him the edge over Will, even though his friend had always been the faster runner of the two. 'What is it?' he called. 'What's wrong?'

'Oh, Robert!' Peggy cried, tears streaming down her face. She gasped for breath, her voice thick with emotion. 'Oh, Robert!' she repeated. 'Come quickly! It's Father!'

Chapter 24

Mrs Barnforth left the village soon after. On the day the village celebrated VE Day she was there, but by the next morning, the house was empty.

Few were upset to hear of her leaving, especially after word spread that her husband had been secretly working for Nazis. *Good riddance to bad news*, some had said. *She always been a bad apple*, said others, but everyone agreed her departure left a pleasant taste in the mouth and was a cause for further celebration.

An opening for someone to oversee the running of the land was now the topic of the village, and discussions were extensive. Despite Ravenscroft House and its estate being handed to the Parish Council, *to be divided up between the farmsteads as the community sees fit*, it seemed that for the present time the Ravenscroft estate was to be managed by one of its own, and the vote was unanimous.

Betty Atkins moved into Ravenscroft House a few days later, the opportunity unexpected but insisted upon by members of the village. The cottage they currently occupied was far too small, and with Will and Robert topping-and-tailing in one bedroom, Maude and Peggy in another, and Barbara forced to share with Betty until she found somewhere new for the three of them to live, the timing could not have been more perfect. With an empty house able to accommodate everyone, why shouldn't they move in? *And anyway, who better to manage farms than Betty Atkins?* people had said. *She's fair worker that lass and pretty much be 'andling job as it is. Treats people wi' respect too.*

Will and Maude had run excitedly from room to room, the house's emptiness suddenly filled with the noise and life it had been missing under Mrs Barnforth, but Peggy and Robert stood back. Ravenscroft House held dark memories for them, and Robert avoided standing in the hall where Mrs Barnforth had first struck him. He would eventually find his way around his emotions, but for now, it brought back feelings he had believed long-buried.

Peggy took his hand. It was not something she had done recently. Her brother was growing up and objected to Peggy treating him like a child, but this time he welcomed her touch unchallenged. 'Memories fade,' she said quietly, her eyes watching her brother's face for any trace of emotion. 'Mrs Barnforth will fade too. She was mean and horrible and nobody liked her, but she's gone now. I know you can't forget what she did, but you need to release those memories and put them away or she will haunt you forever.' She paused and let go of his hand. 'You need to do that.'

'She be right,' said Betty. 'I won't forget night you ended up wi' us, an' you won't forget what 'appened, but time heals. Tha' needs to put past to bed or you'll ne'er get past it.'

Mother placed her hands on Robert's shoulders. 'You listen to Betty,' she said. She could not even begin to understand the pain her son had been through, and her eyes had filled with tears at the truths she had been told. She understood why Robert had reacted the way he had, and although it had not been the behaviour she had brought him up to show, she did not condone it either. Had she come face-to-face with Mrs Barnforth she would have given 'that woman' such a piece of her mind she would never be able to look Barbara Cotterill in the face again. How dare she look down upon her children in such a way! Barbara's anger boiled, but her son did not need to see that.

Robert nodded. Mother was right. Everyone was right. After their bad experiences during the first few years he felt at home now, so why should he let such a vindictive and mean-spirited woman destroy the happiness he felt? It was time to bury the past and move on.

Robert pulled the remains of the needle from his pocket. He had done his best to straighten it, but it held little of its original colour and shape now and he feared it had lost a little of its magic. He balanced it in the palm of his hand as he had on the day his father had first presented him with it, a gift given in love for a son to believe in and to remember his father by.

And at that, Bernard Cotterill reached around his son and placed his hand atop the needle, sealing it between their palms as he had first done, five years before.

Epilogue

Sir Raven stood within the shadow of Carrion's Wood, the afternoon cooler now after the unseasonal temperatures. He had spent the day walking the paths and found the trees calm, their movements in keeping with the light breath of wind that rustled their leafy branches. *As they should be*, he reminded himself.

The stone wall separated to allow him to step through, and he stopped to rest upon it. He was in no rush. He had overseen the secrets buried within Carrion's Wood since the dark days of the world, so what did another day matter? As long as the bloodline of Arthur Pendragon and the legend of the round table endured, woven throughout history like a gossamer thread, he would know his lifelong commitment had been worthwhile. Such knowledge had been entrusted to him alone, with those who had been present to witness recent events retaining no lasting memory once they had stepped beyond the boundary wall. The ancient trees and the spirits which inhabited them had seen to that.

He pondered the knights' reaction to the boy's presence. It was not something he had witnessed since the glorious days of Camelot, an altogether different time when respect and honour had walked hand-in-hand under Arthur's rule. It had opened his eyes to the simple truth that the blood of a king will always be the blood of a king, no matter how many generations may pass.

Sir Raven de Praye twisted the base of his staff into the long grass at his feet as he pondered a shared destiny: his to protect the boy and his descendants; the boy's, or his descendants yet to come, to one day have the honour of leading the Knights of Arthur into battle. For now, the truth of Robert's family line remained known only to Sir Raven de Praye, Knight of Camelot, Protector of the Birthright of Arthur Pendragon, High King of the Ancient Britons. Under his protection, such a truth would remain hidden until the knights awoke to ride out once more beneath the banner of their king.

The darkest hour of all was yet to come.

But not today.

Some day.

Author's Note

This book has had two lives.

Originally conceived in September 2018, the first draft was disregarded when the story took off in a direction I had not intended. Two years later, as Covid 19 and the first UK lockdown took hold, and as I proofread a manuscript for a fellow writer, I found my thoughts returning to my shelved story. It wasn't something I had ever envisaged revisiting, but after a read-through and a severe trim I believed I had something worth developing. By the end of the year I found myself with a completed manuscript, and from there matters took their own course.

The legend of King Arthur and the Knights of the Round Table has fascinated the world for generations, but the location of Camelot, if there is any truth at all in the legend, remains a mystery. Likewise, Arthur's brotherhood of knights varies in number between 12 and 1600, depending on whose account you refer to. For the purpose of this story I have limited the number to 12, using the most frequently occurring knights in nearly all accounts of the legend: Arthur Pendragon; Sir Lancelot; Sir Gawain; Sir Geraint; Sir Percival; Sir Bors the Younger; Sir Lamorak; Sir Kay Gareth; Sir Lamorak; Sir Gaheris; Sir Galahad and Sir Tristan.

The round table at Winchester has no link with Arthur, being an imitation created under Henry III in the 13th Century.

SO44 is a figment of this author's imagination, but Hitler's quest for artefacts of power was indeed true. My novel *Shadow From A Distant Sun* explores the conflict between Captain Joseph Hammerton and Strass in more detail.

While Carrion's Wood and the village of Ravenscroft are both fictional, the woodland has its origins in a hilltop plantation spied from a window on the Darlington to Edinburgh line. Alongside it stood the weathered remains of a guard's railway carriage, an early concept for Carrion's home before it became a stone structure. Most other locations are indeed real, as are a number of the plot points within it: for example, the lady who was plucked from the rubble as a child when her home was bombed; the evacuee who was convinced a man staying in the same guest house she had been sent to live in was a spy, and the elderly gentleman who recollected a fighter skimming the beach towards him, its pilot waving before realization dawned that it was an enemy aircraft. Such stories are the lifeblood of a writer, and I am indebted to every person who took the time to share their memories and experiences with me. Every story was valuable, whether its truth was changed and whether it found its way into the pages of the book or not.

I would like to pay particular thanks to my parents, Francis and Jacqueline Jowsey, who added so much colour to my childhood with stories of their upbringing, their memories of the war and their experiences of growing up during hard times. To Violet Thornborogh, whose experiences as an evacuee provided a detailed account of life away from home. To my brother in ink, John Clewarth, for all things writing and editing, and to the real John Reed, my painting buddy at Gallery TS1 and the voice on my shoulder when it came to character development and plot. To everyone else who has contributed, no matter how large or small, I thank you deeply.

Additional thanks go to my test readers, John Clewarth, John and Linda Reed, Hannah Connelly, Katie Elvin and Ashton Poole, and to everyone who has listened to me ramble on about 'my book'. And finally, to my dear wife Dianne and daughter Ellie-May, for putting up with my writing. Again.

About The Author

David Jowsey was born and raised in Middlesbrough, where he continues to live and work. He studied Visual Arts at Bretton Hall College of Higher Education, Wakefield, graduating in 1988, and after a career in teaching now works for the NHS. He continues to paint and is an active member of the Gallery TS1 group of artists.

To find out more and to view David's writing and artwork, visit www.facebook.com/davidjowseyartist
or visit his website at www.davidjowsey.com

Contact David at: davidjowseyartist@hotmail.com

Also by David Jowsey

DRAGONS IN THE SKY

Set in England and told through the eyes of ten-year-old Tom Richards, *Dragons in the Sky* weaves together the crash of a mysterious object at Roswell in 1947 with a strange shadowy figure, and the rich local history of the Cleveland Hills.

On a blisteringly hot summer day, Tom's world is turned upside down as an incoherent figure stumbles into his garden. He is Danny, a long-lost childhood friend of Tom's father. When Danny begins revealing the story of his youth, Tom's family is forced into an experience none of them could have imagined. Visited by strange beings and terrified beyond their worst nightmares, the family struggles to come to terms with the visions they have witnessed.

As strange events start to unfold, Tom will realise he has a very important role to play.

"Dragons in the Sky is an amazing adventure set against the most vivid backdrop of the moors. Atmospheric, frightening and yet most thrilling – a book that must be read."

GP Taylor, international best-selling author of Shadowmancer and The Curse of Salamander Street.

Available in paperback and e-book format from Amazon

David Jowsey

The sequel to *Dragons in the Sky*

SHATTERED TRUTHS:
THE PAST HIDES A SECRET

MARS 2039

Tom Richards knows he has been destined to visit the red planet since his childhood encounter with the An'Tsari thirty years before.

As part of an international team of astronauts, Tom explores the surface of Mars.

Now, as the crew struggle to survive a planet-wide storm, Tom must confront the existence of a sinister organisation and come to terms with his own future.

Can he protect humanity from a dark and treacherous past, or will the existence of such an overwhelming power mean the extinction of the human race?

"Science Fiction at its best."
The Times Educational Supplement

Available in paperback and e-book format from Amazon

The prequel to *Dragons in the Sky*
and *Shattered Truths*

SHADOW FROM A DISTANT SUN

He was one of Hitler's Right-hand men.
Ruthless. Sinister. He was a shadow of pure evil.
And now he's back.

Summer 1976

The horrors of World War Two are long past, but Joseph Hammerton remains haunted by the lives lost under his command as he hunted a Nazi general known as The White Wolf.

When his Grandad's secret military past is mistakenly uncovered, Danny Forbes' world is suddenly a more exciting place. But then mysterious shadows disturb his dreams, and everything he knows begins to fall apart.

Bonded by trust, Grandfather and Grandson find themselves shoulder to shoulder as they face down an age-old enemy, and attempt to hold back the rise of an ancient evil that threatens the peace of the entire world once more.

Available in paperback and e-book format from Amazon

A true story of personal discovery

WHATEVER HAPPENED TO TWITCH MORGAN?

Growing up with a condition I knew nothing about, I was confused. Doctors called it Tourette's Syndrome, others called it a twitch, but what did that mean, and why did I find myself compelled to utter strange sounds and make jerking movements that drew unwanted attention?

What was happening to my childhood, and would these unwelcome episodes ever go away?

For years, Tourette's Syndrome was a dark stain on my life, but over time I realised it had grown into something far more helpful than I could ever have imagined; something which was about to take my life along unexpected and unfamiliar paths, leaving me more fulfilled than I had ever thought possible.

'An approachable and uplifting story
of life with Tourette's Syndrome.'
www.tourettes-action.org.uk

Available in paperback and e-book format from Amazon

Printed in Great Britain
by Amazon

84365492R00119